City The Son

Samrat Upadhyay is the author of *Arresting God in Kathmandu*, a Whiting Award winner, *The Royal Ghosts*, and *The Guru of Love*, a New York Times Notable Book and a San Francisco Chronicle Best Book of the Year. He has written for *The New York Times* and has appeared on BBC Radio and National Public Radio. Upadhyay is the Martha C. Kraft Professor of Humanities at Indiana University.

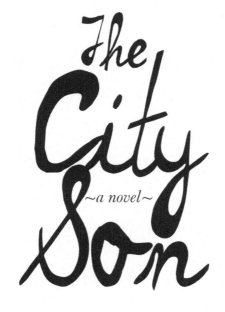

The City

~a novel~

Son

SAMRAT UPADHYAY

RUPA

Published by
Rupa Publications India Pvt. Ltd 2014
7/16, Ansari Road, Daryaganj
New Delhi 110002

Sales centres:
Allahabad Bengaluru Chennai
Hyderabad Jaipur Kathmandu
Kolkata Mumbai

First published in the USA by Soho Press, Inc. 853 Broadway,
New York in 2014

ISBN: 978-81-291-3523-0

First impression 2014

10 9 8 7 6 5 4 3 2 1

Interior design by Janine Agro, Soho Press, Inc.

Printed at Replika Press Pvt. Ltd., India

For Babita and Shahzadi

THE
CITY SON

PART 1

CHAPTER ONE

A STRANGER COMES to the village and delivers the news.

Didi hears a woman's voice in her yard. She's upstairs, going through the boys' old clothes, deciding which ones she wants to keep and which ones to pass down to a neighbor's children. Her first thought when she hears the woman's voice is that something has happened to her husband in the city. Then she knows it's something else. She stands still, holding in her hands a pair of dark blue shorts, too tight for her older son, Amit. "Is anybody home?" the woman cries out again. Didi goes to the window.

"Are you the woman named Sulochana?"

Didi nods.

"I have to talk about an important matter."

The woman identifies herself as belonging to the next village, then she makes some connections—throws out some names—that form a vague picture in Didi's mind about who she is. A sickly feeling has started in Didi's stomach. She doesn't want to hear this woman. I should shut this window, she thinks, and I can go back to sorting my boys' clothes. But there is no going back.

"Sometimes I feel like my heart is going to break," the Masterji wrote in a letter not too long ago, "at the thought of not being able to come home again this year. My heart is going to shatter into pieces—that's what I feel. But this separation is not for long, Sulochana. Next year I am sure to visit." Didi had squinted at the words, mumbling them to herself for coherence; she had studied only up to seventh grade. At home he never called her by her name, but in all his letters he addressed her as "Sulochana." In the evening when the boys had come home, she'd told them, "Next year. He can't come this year—too many students. That's what you get for having a brilliant father." She'd formed her own picture of the name her husband had amassed in the city: people greeted him when he strolled the streets. Each dawn when the air was fresh and vibrant, he made rounds of the temples. His forehead smeared with *tika*, he returned to his neighborhood, drank tea in his favorite shop before going to the school where he taught in the morning session. He returned home around noon and soon thereafter received his first students, to whom he gave his private tutoring. Sons and daughters of high-ranking officials lined up at his door to seek his assistance.

"The other day, the prime minister's wife came to see if I could tutor her nephew," he'd written. "I told her that she ought to have sent someone to fetch me, but she said that she didn't want to disturb me when I was hammering away and chiseling the shape of young minds. Hadn't the king himself often said that the youth of today are the nation builders of tomorrow? She observed the four students I was tutoring at the moment, all of whom were staring at her slack jawed, and said that four nation builders were already in the making. Sulochana! The prime minister's wife! What did I do to deserve this luck? Sometimes I feel that I don't even deserve you and the boys. How patient you have been with me in this absence, this *peeda* of our long separation."

Peeda: she loved the word he used for his torture. *Peeda* was what she felt, too, except she never expressed it.

The sickly feeling carries a smell that rises from her stomach to her mouth. It's like the odor of an animal. The shorts she holds in her hands have a urine spot that has not completely washed away. What's going to happen to my boys? she reflects. But it's too late, and she knows it. She's not at the start of this momentum; she's already in the middle of it. The boys are going to suffer. Other people, unknown faces she hasn't yet met, are going to suffer—people who are now suddenly connected to her.

"Are you going to invite me in?" the woman asks.

"Whatever you need to say, feel free to say from the yard."

"The matter is a bit too delicate for the open air."

"It's okay."

"*Kasto kura nabujheko bhanya.* It's for your sake I'm urging privacy."

"I perfectly understand. Either tell me right here or go your own way."

The woman looks annoyed, but then she begins to speak. Her manner of speaking is singsongy, as if she were reciting a favorite ditty from her childhood.

The woman finishes speaking her main bit, pauses, then continues, "I wouldn't have gone through the trouble of coming here and talking to you had I not been told that you have been kept in the dark about this for years now. How is that possible? I asked myself. How is it that a wife would not know about this big a secret her husband has kept in the city? What kind of wife would not know this? Then I had to see for myself what kind of wife. Now that I have seen you, I know you don't deserve it. What woman does? You have given your life to your husband, haven't you, Sulochanaji? And look at the news that I have brought you.

"I've seen the boy walk hand in hand with his mother in the market. The boy has immaculately smooth skin and perfectly dimpled cheeks and large, curious eyes. His mother is also exceptionally beautiful. Like an actress in a film, that kind of beauty. A city kind of beauty, *sahariya* type, the type one finds in magazines. Her face is longish and perfectly shaped. She is petite, loves to wear red. Apsara is her name. Yes, a nymph—that's what her parents named her. She was a student of his. She came to his flat for tutoring so she could pass the SLC and college exams. Then one day she didn't return home. Her parents disowned her; her brother came to thrash your husband. But she told everyone her place was with him in that sparse flat in the crumbling house in the busy intersection of the city's core.

"When I saw her she was dressed in a shimmering red sari as though she had been wedded that very day. The whole street was glowing because of her. People stopped to look at her, then at her son. You know where this was? Right in the Asan market. Soon you'll know what kind of place Asan is. It's very close to Bangemudha, where your husband lives, near the large wooden lump studded with coins. People say nailing coins into that wood has a palliative function, but I can't remember what it cures. Stomachache? Toothache? This is the type of neighborhood where small bands of men with flowers in their hair and cymbals and drums pass through—amazing how only three or four men with their instruments make the sky throb. Not too long after the boy was born, your husband decided that the one-room flat wasn't big enough, and now they've moved to a small house with a separate kitchen and an indoor bathroom. It's not a bad place. The rent is more expensive than the previous flat, but then your husband is also getting more students to tutor now.

"In the Asan market that day, the boy's mother was smiling at everyone. The boy was sucking on an ice cream. His beauty made my heart ache, Sulochanaji. I was told that the boy's mother never wore anything other than bright red—bright red sari, bright red blouse with dhoti—as though it were the festival of Teej all year long. When she was pregnant with the boy, she put a big red *tika* on her forehead, I was told, and with her rouge and her red *sindur* smeared on the parting in her hair, she was like a radiant flame. There are these dental shops in Bhedasingh with their horrendous wares—hammers and wrenches and pliers and whatnots—near where your husband lives. When she passed by, those dentists came to the doors of their shops to admire her. They teased her, despite their wives looking from the windows above. '*Sahuni,*' they said—they called her *sahuni,* even though she didn't operate any shops—'where are you off to so early in the morning, wearing such nice clothes?'

"'*Ooo tyahi samma jana lageko.* I have to buy a thing or two.'

"'And you are leaving poor Masterji by himself?'

"'He is tutoring his students.'

"The wives of these dentists also called out to her, 'So, *sahuni,* when is the big guest coming?' Apsara wasn't showing at that time, but somehow the whole neighborhood guessed, correctly, that the boy was on his way. The eyes of these dental wives followed her as she moved on. They wondered about the Masterji's family back in the village. They invited Apsara up for tea and sweets and plied her with questions. She feigned ignorance when the dental wives asked about the wife and sons in the village."

Since she has been talking for so long, the messenger's mouth is dry, and she holds on to the hope that Didi will offer her some water. But Didi has already left the window. It's twilight. The woman thinks she should be on her way back. Drunks appear on the village pathways after dark; there have been cases of rape. Just as the woman is about to turn away from the house, Didi appears at the door.

CHAPTER TWO

DIDI IS HOLDING a cup of tea. She hands it to the woman.

"Shall we sit down for a while?" the woman says, moved by this unexpected gesture of kindness. "My legs are giving out on me."

Didi leads her to the porch, where there's a mat. Darkness is beginning to fall around them. The boys will soon return home from their play. Didi will have to cook rice. There are some leftover vegetables from this morning. There's some milk—she keeps two cows in the shed in the back—and a neighbor has brought over some goat hooves, which she will boil to make broth for the boys.

"What are you going to do?" the woman asks.

"I'm going tomorrow."

"What about the boys?"

"They're going with me."

"Will you tell them?"

"They'll find out soon enough."

Didi is looking into the dark, perhaps to listen to her sons' voices. Someone walks by on the path with a torch and calls out her name. "Everything is well, *bhauju?*" It's a man's voice.

"Everything is well."

"What is the Masterji's news in the city?"

"Everything is well."

The man bids her goodbye and moves on.

"I saw them with my own two eyes," the woman says.

"Did you see him there, my husband, in that marketplace?"

"No, but I did some investigating. I went to Bange-mudha, knocked on the door, pretended that I was a student seeking help. Me, a grown woman! But I said I was what they now call an adult learner, returning to education after a long time."

"What does the new flat look like?"

"It's right next to the street, just a stone's throw away from where he used to live, where she came to him for tutoring, where the beautiful boy, Tarun, was born."

"I want to see this boy," Didi says.

"This flat is the whole house, one story. The owner is a local merchant."

"Tell me about Asan, since this is the place where you saw the boy and his mother."

"It's the old part of the city, you know, so it has that charm of the olden, golden days."

"I know nothing of the city. I'm just a village numskull. So please tell me everything."

"There is a vegetable market which is rancorous and alive all day. Spice shops make you sneeze as you pass by. Oil men sit in their cubbies dripping in oil, and they have these long, thin ladles they use to scoop the oil and pour it into their customers' containers. There's the famous temple of Annapurna. You might want to pay her your respects before you go to your husband's home. There's also a spot in Asan where a fish fell from the sky a long time ago. You can still see its imprints, but that's a long story."

Just then the boys come home, fighting. The older, louder one is berating the younger one, who is whining. They stop when they see the silhouette of the woman.

"I should get moving," the woman says.

"How will you make your way at night? You can leave early in the morning."

The woman sleeps next to Didi. The boys, snoring loudly, sleep in the corner. Because it's a new place, the woman keeps waking up every hour or so, and every time she senses that Didi hasn't slept. Toward early morning, she asks Didi, "What are you thinking about?"

"I can't stop thinking about that beautiful boy."

CHAPTER THREE

"*RAMRI CHHAINA,*" a villager had warned the Masterji when his father finalized his marriage to Didi. "She has a regrettable face," the Masterji overheard someone say. Yet every time the Masterji thought of approaching his father about what he'd heard, he lost his nerve. His father had suffered hardships so the Masterji could go to the city for his studies. His father had eaten only one meal a day; he had taken out loans.

Masterji's father would have been happy to have him stay in the village, but his teachers had been encouraging him to opt for further studies in the city. "Don't waste that fine brain of yours," they said. Right after his School Leaving Certificate exams, in which he performed brilliantly, he had begun to teach at the school where he had studied. Although he enjoyed stimulating those young minds, he was slowly becoming restless. In the midst of imparting the day's lesson he'd look out of the window and see his time passing by without any direction. The streams and paddy fields and woods where he had played now began to appear like a giant trap, the hills like a tomb closing in on him. Finally he went to his father, who said, "Of course, I support your decision and will make the necessary arrangements."

"The city will be expensive."

"That's not your concern. You go there and study and become a big man and make us all proud. Just one thing, though."

"Yes, Father?"

"Don't forget your village. This is the place that gave you birth. You should never forget where you were born, the people around you when you were growing up."

"Yes, Father."

"Don't get lost in the way of the city, Son."

After four years of studying for his BA in Kathmandu, the Masterji came out at the top of his class. When his father called him home to get married, he returned, and now he was despondent at the news of his bride's ugliness.

One morning the Masterji embarked upon a two-hour walk to his future bride's village. He had her name and the name of her father, and after some inquiries he located her house. Given the two-story structure and an outer façade of nice-looking bricks, he knew that this was a family of decent wealth, something his father had already hinted at. The Masterji sat in a tea shop across from the house and watched it. For nearly an hour he watched, drawing questionable glances from the *sahuni*. Then his bride emerged with an empty *gagri* on her waist. She was going to fetch water. She was round, her face like a soccer ball. His heart dropped in disappointment. When she came closer, he saw her face. It was *bhadda*, flat and dark and uninteresting. Her cheeks were puffed up as though cotton had been stuffed inside. She had dark spots on her face. A neighbor of hers passed by, and his bride began talking with her.

The Masterji asked the *sahuni*, "Is that the girl of the house? Sulochana?"

"Yes, that's her. Do you know her?"

"I've heard of her, that's all."

"If you like her," the *sahuni* said, "it's too late. She's about to get married."

"I see."

"Are you surprised? Given how ugly and round she is?"

"I'm just here drinking tea."

"They've been wanting to get her married for a while, but all the boys have balked. But now they've found some poor sod. A bright fellow in the city, I hear." The *sahuni* laughed. "He has no idea what he's getting into. I hear the boy's father has taken some big loan from this girl's family, and the marriage is an exchange."

The Masterji sipped his tea.

"Would you want to spend day and night with that face?"

"She must have some virtues."

"She's a good girl, works hard, a good cook. A model wife. But that face! What does it remind you of?"

The Masterji shrugged.

"No, no, tell me. Does it remind you of something?"

The Masterji said nothing.

"A battered *bhakundo*, like the football our local boys kick and kick so hard on the field that it's all blackened and bruised."

The Masterji paid the *sahuni* and said, "You're no beauty either," as he left. As he walked past his bride, the Masterji noted that her lower right arm, not covered by her dhoti, resembled an elephant's trunk.

The Masterji trudged back home on the narrow paths of the hills. There were several moments during that journey when he could have swerved onto a different route, descended to a different village, then perhaps a few more villages until he reached a place from where a bus could carry him into the plains, where he could have disappeared. But he went home and helped his father prepare for the wedding.

Once they got married, the Masterji gradually came to appreciate his wife, even though he spent most of the year in the city. Despite all the cruel comments that had been flung her way throughout her life, she was even tempered and hardworking. She took care of the Masterji's father as he became increasingly feeble and sickly. She spoon-fed him and bathed him with a towel. She was ferocious in bed, during those times when the Masterji visited. She was like a tigress who took immediate control. She clawed and scratched and was inexhaustible. When the Masterji got tired, she rode him, with abandon, uncaring of the noise—the rocking, the crunching, the moans, and the whimpers. She made him cry, gasp, and, occasionally, shout—so loud and rollicking was their lovemaking. She was bigger than he, and he had always been thin and academic looking, so when she climbed on top he became a little afraid. During those perspiring nights, she didn't tolerate any excuse or demurring from him. Her physical prowess was so strong that had he made a false move she'd have surely struck him. The pleasures he experienced those nights—her ample thighs and arms enveloping him, smothering him—were so severe that in the morning, once she became quiet and respectful like a traditional housewife, he wondered if he had dreamed them.

"This type of daughter-in-law only the most supremely blessed people will get in their homes," the Masterji's father said in his croaky, throaty voice. To his father, his daughter-in-law was an embodiment of Goddess Durga herself, strong yet sweet, firm yet nurturing. His father thought the bedroom noises were good signs. He saw the depleted yet satisfied face of the Masterji in the morning and thought her lack of beauty was no longer an issue.

But while the Masterji returned to the city happy and contented, mixed in with this satisfaction was a small degree of anxiety about who she was. If I displease her—this thought came to him swiftly, like a small, fast sparrow—she will crush me. In the city the anxiety stayed with him, and it gradually diminished because their distance was so great. But over the years, each time he boarded the bus for the village, he experienced an excited type of dread. He didn't look forward to seeing her face, but his mind went into a frenzy thinking what she'd do to him at night. Even when he returned for the last rites for his father, she didn't leave him alone at night. It was not the proper thing to do—the grieving period was supposed to be pure and uncontaminated—and he felt guilty when he returned to the city.

After the birth of their first son, Amit, her body became heavier, and rounder, and she ate twice the amount she had before. He hated the way she ate, opening her mouth wide like a hippopotamus and shoveling her food in with her hand. Her jaws made loud chomping sounds when she ate, but he was afraid to say anything. He wondered if he had been spoiled by the city, as his father had warned, but he could no longer stand the noises she made, for example, when she gargled in the morning—the *aakh* and the *thhoo* that went on for eternity. They began to appear uncouth to him, crass and hillbilly.

CHAPTER FOUR

A FEW DAYS later Didi appears with Amit and Sumit in tow in Bangemudha at the Masterji's new flat. The boys run to their father, who tousles their hair and comments on how they've grown since he last saw them.

"You should have informed me," he tells them after they enter the house with their trunks and their bundles. The beautiful boy and his mother, the Masterji's city wife, have gone to her mother's, and he's expecting them to arrive any minute now. Perhaps he can take Didi and his two sons to another location, offer an excuse about why they can't stay here. "My students will be arriving here shortly," he complains.

"We came a long way on the bus," Didi says. The boys

are looking out of the window at the neighbor's house, where some children are flying a kite on the roof. The Masterji thinks of lines from a famous poet that speak of the neighborhood in chaos after a child falls out of a window.

"There's not even food in the house to eat," the Masterji says. "Perhaps for tonight you and the boys—"

"Food is here." Didi turns her back to him, kneels, and opens the trunk, from where she proceeds to extract various items: flattened rice, *anarsa* and *sel* for the Masterji's sweet tooth, and some fruits. Amit reaches into his bag and pulls out a wooden container filled with *mohi*, the buttermilk splashing inside, another village staple that's the Masterji's favorite.

"Do you want some?" Amit says, and his father detects a hint of mockery in his voice.

When Tarun and his mother, Apsara, arrive about an hour later, Didi is cooking in the kitchen, her back to them. She doesn't turn to look. Amit and Sumit are playing a game of snakes and ladders in the corner, and they stop, their eyes first on Apsara, then on Tarun. The Masterji is sitting on the bed. Apsara pauses in the doorway, her hand holding a bag of spinach she was going to cook. Her instinct is to grab Tarun by his hand and leave. But all she can do is look at the floor, an intruder in her own house. "Come in," the Masterji finally says. "Go," Apsara says to Tarun, who goes to his father, leans against him on the bed. He puts his arm around Tarun, tentatively. Apsara continues to stand in the doorway, her gaze lowered; occasionally when she looks up, it's on Didi's back that her eyes land. Didi is stirring her vegetables and her rice, then she turns and faces Apsara, says, "You must be surprised, to have these uninvited guests in this house."

Apsara shuffles toward Didi, like she's about kneel on the floor and prostrate.

"There was no meat in the house," Didi says, "so it'll just have to be rice and radish today. It's nearly done."

Apsara offers her the bag of spinach.

"Keep it," Didi says. "It looks kind of yellowed anyway."

Apsara sits on her haunches in the kitchen, watching as Didi stirs for a final time, then turns off the stove. Didi ladles some rice and radish onto a plate and tells Amit, "Take the plate to your father." Then she ladles rice and radish for all the children. The children, along with Apsara, sit on the floor next to the bed and eat. For some reason Tarun is hungry that evening and finds everything delicious. His mother picks at her food. The Masterji eats in bed; he is mostly quiet. At one point, he lifts his head and says, "The salt is just right in the radish." Didi doesn't eat, just watches. Her eyes are specially reserved for Tarun, on whom she bestows small, encouraging smiles. Amit and Sumit eat huge mounds of rice, then burp loudly two or three times. Once the Masterji is done, he leaves the plate near Didi and washes his hands and gargles in the sink. Apsara, her meal barely touched, stands and goes to the bathroom, from where she doesn't emerge for an hour.

That night Didi sleeps in a corner with her two sons. Tarun and Apsara sleep in another corner, where Apsara laid bedding for the two of them soon after she emerged, her face weary, from the bathroom. "It's time to sleep," she told Tarun in a low voice. Didi had taken an incredibly long time to eat, and then she had washed the dishes and stacked them by the sink. She had laid her own bedding near the kitchen, where her two boys are now lying. Amit is staring at the ceiling, alert to the movements around the room. He knew, before they boarded the bus to the city, that his father was up to no good, and a hard type of anger had come into his eyes. In the village, people speak of him as a troublemaker. Sumit is reading a musty book belonging to his father. He is a sharp contrast to his brother: always smiling, sweet tempered, soft voiced, ready to acquiesce. He loves to read and is eager to share new things he's learned from his books. The Masterji remains in the same position on the bed. Soon, Didi is snoring with her back to the room, a low but steady snore that threatens to last the night.

Tarun falls asleep, then wakes up a couple of hours later to silence so deep that it feels like a dream. He can see his father's silhouette on the bed—at some point he must have turned off the light. Apsara is also awake. He is thirsty, so he stands and makes his way to the kitchen, where he tilts the *gagro* and pours himself a glass of water. He drinks, facing the room. His glance falls upon Didi, whose eyes are open and observing him. As Tarun returns to his bed, the Masterji reaches out and clasps his arm, like the hand of a ghost in the dark. Then his father lets him go, and the boy returns to his mother.

The Masterji, despite his education and his name, crumples and is cowed by Didi's arrival. Every morning Apsara rouses herself from her bed, ready to battle the day, perhaps to confront her husband or to stand up to Didi, tell her that the Masterji is also her husband, married legitimately in a temple. But her resolve is short-lived. Once she has to face Didi with her buffalo-like presence and her large, staring eyes, Apsara weakens. Didi has taken over the kitchen. With her body language and expressions she suggests that Apsara doesn't know how to cook, that the Masterji thus far has been eating lousy food. Didi dusts in places where there's no dust; she takes the Masterji's mattress out to the yard and beats it ruthlessly. She entrusts her older son, Amit, instead of Apsara, with going to the market to fetch groceries. Within a few days of her arrival, the Masterji is already handing over to Didi the income from his tutees. Apsara hardly gets a moment alone with the Masterji, who avoids being with her alone and refuses to meet her eyes. Whenever she approaches him, his eyes dart toward Didi, who, even with her back turned toward them, knows what is going on. Apsara looks windblown, and she has taken up the habit of wringing her hands, digging her nails into her palms.

At night, Apsara twitches and jerks, her face buried in her pillow. Tarun doesn't know whether she has spoken to anyone at work—she's a teller at a bank—about what has happened at home. One afternoon the neighbor next door, who has a phone, knocks on the door and says that Tarun has a call. Tarun has just returned from school, and Didi has handed him a boiled egg and a glass of milk. The Masterji is tutoring a student on the bed. "He's eating his snacks," Didi says to the neighbor. She feeds Tarun well, as though he's her own child, and on Saturday she takes him out to the yard and gives him a good bath, scrubbing him and rubbing the soap vigorously all over his body, while Apsara watches from the window. He always feels refreshed and lighter afterward.

"Who's on the phone?" Didi asks the neighbor, who mumbles he doesn't know. "Then he won't come," she says. The neighbor watches her worriedly, then says, "It might be his mother. The line was bad, I couldn't tell." Busy with his tutee, the Masterji doesn't hear this conversation.

Didi signals Tarun to go, so he follows the neighbor to his house. "Tarun, call your father to the phone," Apsara whispers when he picks up the phone. "But don't announce it's me." Then, "Where is she?"

"She's in the house," Tarun says. Didi rarely leaves the house; his mother knows that. The neighbor is standing in the doorway, listening. "Didi knows it's you on the phone," Tarun tells his mother.

"I told our neighbor not to announce it's me!" Apsara is breathing hard.

Tarun waits for her instructions. She must have gathered her courage at the other end, because when she speaks her voice is firmer. "Tell your father it's me, and tell him to come to the phone immediately."

"Where are you calling from?"

"From the bank, Tarun, quickly please."

Tarun puts down the phone and brushes past the neighbor to go next door to his house. Didi is doing something in the kitchen, her back as usual to the room. Tarun sits next to his father on the bed, pokes him on the thigh, and says, "Phone next door."

Without looking at him, the Masterji asks, "Phone? For me? Who's calling?"

"It's important."

"Who is it?"

When Tarun doesn't answer, both the Masterji and his tutee look at him.

Tarun's boiled egg and glass of milk are still unconsumed. Amit and Sumit are lounging in their corner bed. They arrived home from school earlier than Tarun and have already eaten their snacks.

Once Tarun's father realizes who's on the phone, his eyes drift toward Didi. "What does she want?" the Masterji whispers to Tarun.

Tarun shakes his head.

The tutee asks the Masterji a question. The Masterji says to Tarun, "Tell her we can talk when she comes home."

Tarun returns to the neighbor's and tells his mother what the Masterji said.

After a pause Apsara says, "Tell him that I'll continue to hold."

When Tarun goes home and informs his father, the Masterji says, "Okay, let me finish this section, then I'll go." Tarun stays with his father, hoping that he'll soon put on his slippers, but the Masterji doesn't get up.

Apsara returns home late in the evening, so subdued that she looks like someone who's just been fired from her job. Since she's also three hours late and it has turned dark outside, everyone has already eaten.

No one mentions the phone call. Apsara changes in the bathroom and comes to bed. The Masterji is already in bed, and only one light burns in the flat. Tarun is lying on his side, reading. Apsara rumples his hair and whispers, "Did you eat?"

Tarun nods.

"There's food for you," Didi says from her corner. "On a plate in the kitchen."

"I'm not hungry," Apsara says.

"Then why do I slave in this house, cooking and cleaning? And he breaks his back teaching, just so we have the luxury of wasting our food?"

Apsara jerks up, rapidly moves toward the kitchen, grabs her plate, and returns to Tarun. She eats, shoving the rice into her mouth in a whimpering, helpless anger. She gags and coughs as she eats.

CHAPTER FIVE

A FEW WEEKS later Apsara finds a flat for the two of them in Kupondole. She doesn't want to go to her parents' house because she doesn't want to admit to anyone her defeat.

The mother and the son live on the second floor of a large building, in a room that overlooks the main street and even provides a glimpse of the Bagmati Bridge and a small section of the river. Apsara enrolls Tarun in an English medium school up the hill in Jawalakhel, so every morning a bus picks him up from outside the building and transports him to school.

A couple of weeks after he begins, his Nepali teacher, a short man with a thick, flat face, asks Tarun, "Is it true that your father left your mother?"

"My mother left him."

"Right, right. But do you visit him, your father?"

Tarun nods.

"Does your father love you?"

Tarun hesitates, then nods. He's sure that his father loves him, but since Didi's and the boys' arrival the Masterji has been uncomfortable showing his affection. Before, he used to take Tarun to Ratna Park, where they kicked around a rubber ball, and he fed his son ice cones from roaming vendors. But after Didi came, his father has become reserved. Now it's Didi who is physically demonstrative. She tousles his hair, wipes his face, and says, "You should have been born my son," even in front of Amit and Sumit and, once, before they moved to Kupondole, with his mother listening.

"I'm sure your father loves you," the teacher says. His smile gets funnier. "And your mother? She must be feeling quite lonely?" He has pulled Tarun to a table in the teachers' lounge to have this conversation. "I have seen your mother. Such a nice-looking woman yet such a sad situation." He flips a pen in his fingers, repeatedly. "I wish I could come to your house to talk to her. What do you think, Tarun? To discuss your studies, your progress. Maybe have a cup of tea? Ha! Ha! *Khair,* it doesn't matter if she doesn't know how to make tea. I will take you two for sweets to Ram Bhandar. You know Ram Bhandar? Yes? I thought so. Ha! Ha! You like sweets, don't you, Tarun? I can tell. *Rasgulla*? *Laddoo*? What else do you like to eat?"

But when Tarun gives his mother the slip of paper on which he has written his teacher's name and a phone number, she stares at the paper and says, "You're so good." She hasn't absorbed anything Tarun has said.

Apsara found work at a bank in Thapathali after they moved to Kupondole. Every morning she crosses the bridge to go to work, and it's good that she doesn't have to venture into the city center, where the chances of running into Didi are high. Apsara has begun mumbling to the stove when she cooks. Some days Tarun finds her talking to the wall; she shakes her head and says, "*Nai, nai,*" or "*Hoina, hoina. Hundaina.*"

One evening, he and his mother are on their way to New Road for a purchase or two before heading home. They were delayed in Kamalachhi, where his school uniform was being sewn. It's getting dark, and Apsara is nervous at being in such close proximity to Bangemudha, near Didi.

In Asan they come upon a gathering. Tarun loves spectacles—magic shows, circuses featuring children doing impossible contortions, street theater—and he tugs at his mother, asking her to stop. "*Late hunchha,* babu," she says. Her eyes dart about, apprehensive. A tremor runs through her body. Sometimes when he holds her hand on the street, he feels something travel up and down her skin—a small dose of terror. It's as though her body is reliving, in intervals throughout the day, her first encounter with Didi. In their new flat in Kupondole when she hunches over the stove, she appears to stop breathing for a few seconds until the current passes through her. Every time this shiver journeys through her, it inflicts a smidgen of damage, so tiny that one would probably have to put it under a microscope to see it, but it's there.

"One moment," he says as he disengages his hand from hers and pushes through the crowd to the front. Lit by bright portable lamps, a figure is dancing. It is wearing a traditional mask of a wrathful god—bulging eyes, thick lips, baring sharp teeth, its face a mélange of colors. The dancer has on a colorful frock and a tunic with frills that sweep the air as he moves. There is music—loud drums and cymbals—but Tarun can't locate the players. The music appears to descend from the sky above and roll over the people. The mask terrifies Tarun, but then at times its eyes appear not angry but kind. Without realizing it—and possibly to escape his near-wailing mother—Tarun has stepped into the clear space allotted to the dancer by his audience. "Babu, *kahan harayau timi? Harey! Yetro bheedma.* Tarun!" But Apsara's voice, muted by the loud crashing and banging around him, doesn't persuade him.

Suddenly the mask cocks its head at Tarun. Then it hurtles toward him and grabs him by the shoulders, its gargantuan eyes thrust against Tarun's face. Tarun screams. The crowd laughs. He pees in his pants. His mother makes her way to him and kneels down in front of him with a gasp, her eyes quickly taking in the wetness of his crotch. She pushes the unmasked dancer away from him, picks him up, and carries him away, gently scolding him as she wipes his mucus-filled nose with her fingers: what possessed him to leave her and go to that lakhey?

Tarun's heart is beating so fiercely it's throbbing in his throat. He closes his eyes, but the mask appears before him, enraged, and he whimpers. As Apsara carries him and hurries through the evening crowd, he can feel the stickiness on his thighs, and, without his wanting it, his penis somewhat hardens. He worries that his mother will feel his rise or notice the small tent in his pants. But caught up in her own anxieties, she notices nothing.

Within weeks after they move to Kupondole, Didi sends the Masterji to fetch Tarun one Saturday. At nine o'clock, when Apsara is cooking and Tarun is engaged in a drawing that he wants to submit for a national competition, there's a knock on the door. "See who it is, babu," Apsara says.

Tarun wonders if it's a neighborhood boy wanting to play, but it's his father, along with Amit and Sumit. Apsara doesn't say anything as the Masterji sits on the bed and motions to his two sons to do the same. He looks around, then his eyes land on Apsara. "So, you've settled in all nicely here?" he asks. "This looks like a nice place."

She sits on her haunches on the floor, next to the stove, her body trembling. "You couldn't come alone?" she says.

"I wanted to show Amit and Sumit their brother's new house."

Amit is watching the two of them carefully. He had instructions from Didi.

"Something delicious is being cooked here, I can tell," the Masterji says. His face is soaked in guilt.

"I don't know how to cook, remember?"

The Masterji laughs sheepishly. "Are you not even going to offer a glass of water? We walked all the way—couldn't catch the bus."

"Even the water I serve stinks," she says, but she gets up and pours some from the corner *gagro*, first for the Masterji, then for Amit and Sumit.

The Masterji drinks long and hard, then, setting the glass on the floor, says, "This place is so close to the shops." When he realizes that she's not going to carry on small talk with him, he addresses Tarun, who's sitting next to his mother, "Tarun, how are things? How is school?"

"Fine."

The Masterji notices Tarun's artwork, a pencil drawing of mountains with a picturesque village ensconced underneath, a big house in the foreground with a smiling family of six—a man, two women, and three boys—holding hands in the yard. "Did you make this?" He picks it up from the floor. "Look!" he shows it to Amit and Sumit. "What a beautiful picture your brother has drawn." Sumit cranes his neck to look, and Amit glances at it, then shoots Tarun a mirthful look.

"I think you are going to be an artist when you grow up!" the Masterji says. To Apsara he says, "I have come to take Tarun with me to Bangemudha."

She lets out a short laugh. "What for?"

"He also needs to spend time with his father."

"What for?"

"Doesn't he need to spend time with his father?"

"You can come and visit him here. When the mood strikes you."

"With my busy schedule, when can I come?"

"Didi has instructed us not to come home without Tarun," Amit says. His words are slow, throaty, like an adult's in conversation with another adult.

She ignores him and tells the Masterji that she'll allow Tarun to live in Bangemudha only over her dead body.

The Masterji looks bedraggled. Tarun remembers that not too long ago his father and his mother sat on their bed in Bangemudha, he with this lungi wrapped around his waist, gazing into her eyes, speaking softly to her. He remembers his father buying gifts for his mother—earrings, a scarf, and the special *titaura* she likes. His father took them on outings, to the Balaju Gardens, to Gokarna, even to the movies.

In the end, it's decided that Tarun will visit Bangemudha every Saturday to spend the afternoon. This will enable him to bond with his brothers and also spend time with his father. Apsara agrees to this with great reluctance, and Amit is angry that he's unable to fulfill Didi's wish that they not return home without Tarun.

CHAPTER SIX

APSARA GOES TO work, crossing the Bagmati Bridge in the morning, but Tarun doesn't know how much work she really does. She has always been a small woman; now she appears to have shriveled even more. The river is raging; it's monsoon, and the waves are striking the shores like they're ready to break something. The boy has swum in this river on Saturdays on his way to Bangemudha. He can't stand what's happening to his mother—the way she is falling apart—and he goes to the river and strips down to his underwear and swims. He's made a couple of friends here, street urchins who are awed by the fact that he lives in a flat, attends a boarding school, and speaks good English, and yet here he is among them, swimming in the river like a common ruffian. He doesn't tell them about his mother. When they ask him where his father is, he tells them that he's gone abroad to work. He pretends Mahesh Uncle is his father, and he tells his river friends that his father travels abroad to countries like Japan and Australia and holds meetings with ambassadors and ministers. Mahesh Uncle has visited the flat two times, and both times he has brought Tarun gifts, at one time a set of colored pens and at another time a box of chocolates. "From Switzerland," he said.

Mahesh Uncle is also worried about Apsara. He is a large-bodied man, large jawed. He is always in suits. Apart from serving on the board of the bank where Apsara works, he owns Mahesh Enterprises, a trading company that imports cigarettes and alcohol and exports handicrafts and carpets. The company also owns a small guesthouse in Thamel, with plans afoot to open up a larger resort-style hotel in the lakeside city of Pokhara. He travels quite a bit—Singapore, Dubai, sometimes Australia and Japan. He breathes heavily, especially when he's standing. He has a kind heart, and the boy needs someone with a kind heart in his life right now.

"*Afno khayl rakhnu parcha,*" Mahesh Uncle says to Apsara. "*Yo ta timro matrai kura hoina ni.* If you neglect yourself, who is going to look after our dear Tarun?" She looks ashamed and embarrassed when he says this. *I can take care of myself,* Tarun wants to tell Mahesh Uncle. *And I can take care of my mother.*

One early evening Mahesh Uncle drops by and becomes distraught to find Apsara asleep in bed, facing the wall. Tarun is doing his homework. Apsara doesn't even realize that Mahesh Uncle has come and that he has noticed the empty stove. When Tarun tried to wake her up after school, she had mumbled and moaned but had not woken up. He had looked around for the usual packet of Arrowroot biscuits he snacked on until his mother cooked dinner, but there were no biscuits. He could have gone next door and asked for some food from the neighbor, but he was too embarrassed, so he sucked on a piece of an old candy he found in his pocket and settled down to do his homework.

Mahesh Uncle has come because Apsara has begun to accumulate quite a number of absences, and her immediate supervisor is unhappy, and her colleagues critical; they complain that she has a free rein because she has a patron on the board of directors. They say "patron" sarcastically, but Tarun knows there's nothing between Mahesh Uncle and his mother. Every now and then, however, Tarun pretends there's something. When Mahesh Uncle sits next to his mother's bed and talks to her, for example, he imagines Mahesh Uncle reaching out with his pudgy fingers to stroke her forehead and chase away all her worries. Mahesh Uncle does touch her forehead but more like a father might do to a daughter. The age difference between her and Mahesh Uncle is great enough that on occasion Tarun thinks Mahesh Uncle could be his grandfather. Tarun hasn't had a relationship with his grandparents, only occasional gifts, visits during certain festivals. When Tarun was born, his grandparents had come to Bangemudha, somber and wary. It was their first visit to the flat, and they were not pleased with the small bed, the cramped corner that also served as the kitchen, the bare-essential pots and pans, the constant stream of noise from the street—honks, yells, laughter, cycle bells, temple bells, hawker wails—a far cry from the lawned house in Naxal where one has to walk at least a block before encountering a street with traffic. But by that time they had resigned themselves to their daughter's inexplicable, scandalous act.

Over the years they have grudgingly accepted Tarun as a child of the strange union between their daughter and a married man. When he visits them, his grandparents treat him like a distant relative. In their house there are no photos of him or his mother after she married the Masterji. All the photos of his mother in his grandparents' house in Naxal are of the pre-Masterji days: she is in her tight flared pants, in red high-heeled shoes.

But the sudden exit of Tarun and his mother from Bangemudha after Didi's arrival has devastated his grandparents, who have severed all contact. Their shame about their daughter is so great that the only way they can cope with it is by pretending she, and Tarun, are not in their lives anymore.

"You can't go on like this." Mahesh Uncle's voice is gently reproachful this evening in Kupondole. Apsara sits up groggily and attempts to gather herself. "Come, let's go out and eat," Mahesh Uncle says. She responds in a small voice that she doesn't wish to be seen in public. "Then we'll go to my house," Mahesh Uncle says, refusing to bow to her stubbornness. Finally, she stands—Tarun helps her get up on her feet as though she were an invalid—and washes her face in the corner sink. The sari she's been sleeping in has wrinkled. The three of them go down, where his car is waiting.

If not for Mahesh Uncle, Tarun thinks, his mother could have died. In the case of her premature death, Tarun would have gone to Bangemudha to live with his father, with Didi and Amit and Sumit. When he first imagines this, it seems strange to Tarun, the idea of living with his father and his village family. Bangemudha is where he grew up, but now it feels like an alien place when he visits, as though he'd only dreamed that he'd spent his childhood there. In Bangemudha, when he stands next to the bed where he's slept all these years with his father and mother, the bed looks different. He feels awkward in the Bangemudha house, and his father appears like a distant uncle, even though the Masterji calls his name extra sweetly when he visits on Saturdays.

Amit is hostile to Tarun and bullies him. Whenever he gets a chance, he looks around, then pinches Tarun or hits him on the shoulder, hard. "*Muji,*" he whispers, "*randi ko chhoro.*" Amit is thin and taut and strong. Tarun has borne the brunt of that strength when Amit has physically tackled him. Amit looks for an excuse to fight, then suddenly

Tarun is tackled to the ground; Amit sits on him, his legs
straddling Tarun, his fingers clamping Tarun's wrists. It's as
if a boy made of iron has sat on Tarun. One time when
Amit pinned Tarun to the ground in the yard he brought
his mouth close to his and said, "Open your mouth." When
Tarun did, Amit spat into it. "*La, muji, mero thuk nil!*" He
let go. Sumit was standing, watching, smiling, but he wasn't
smiling at what had happened; he was just smiling his sweet
smile. Was Didi watching? Tarun's eyes fell on the window
of the kitchen, where she was, but the figure inside was
too blurred for him to know whether she'd seen anything.
"How's that mother of yours?" Amit frequently asks him,
then laughs. Somehow Tarun doesn't feel like arguing with
him or resisting him when he bullies him or even when he
calls Apsara names. It's as though Tarun has granted Amit
the right to antagonize him.

The person Tarun is beginning to feel the most connected to in Bangemudha is Didi. "My beautiful son,"
she says. "Look how beautiful our Tarun is," she says in
front of everyone, and Tarun can feel Amit's dagger eyes on
him. They sit on the carpet on the floor next to the bed,
where the Masterji sits. He's aged since Didi has arrived.
He smiles at Tarun, as though delighted by the love Didi is
showing toward him. But his eyes are constantly checking
Didi's face, gauging her moods. When she's pleased, and
she's often pleased when Tarun visits, he relaxes. But most
of the time his face is taut, tense as though he is expecting someone to come from the side and strike him a blow.

Tarun is reminded of the adage his Nepali teacher likes to repeat: *Agultole haneko kukur bijuli chamkida tarsinchha.* It fits Tarun's father: he is indeed like the mutt who, once someone hits him with firewood, winces every time lightning strikes the sky.

Didi's fingers caress Tarun's face, his chin. "I think he's the most beautiful boy in the whole world," she says, her gaze fixed on him.

"Eh, beautiful boy!" Amit calls him when everyone's out of earshot. "Eh, beautiful boy, *randi ko chhora.*"

Tarun loves the food Didi cooks: *kheer, malpua, haluwa,* and an assortment of sweet stuff. Increasingly she seems to cook just for him. "I made this especially for my son today," she says as she puts a plate of his favorite snack in front of him. She watches as he eats. Sometimes she gives him more food than she gives her own two sons, as though she knows that he hasn't been eating well in Kupondole. Didi never asks him about his mother. Once or twice he's had the urge to blurt it all out to Didi. She will understand what he's going through. She'll wipe his tears with her palm, kiss him, then lead him to the tap where she'll wash his face, her thick, stubby fingers vigorously eliminating all remnants of pain and suffering, then set him down on the floor and ask him what he wants to eat. After he's had his fill, she'll pull him into her lap and massage his head, her fingers gentle and caressing, and as he feels drowsy, she'll murmur into his ears, words that he doesn't understand but that are nonetheless pleasant. He'll squirm in her lap, and she'll stroke his back, his buttocks. She may even murmur, "Why does my son need to go home tonight? Why doesn't he stay the night here, with his Didi?" And half drowsy, he'll smile, for spending the night here in Bangemudha, cuddled next to Didi, appeals to him greatly.

If it were up to Didi, she'd keep Tarun in Bangemudha. "That so-called mother of his will starve him to death," Didi says to the Masterji. "Look at my Tarun, all skin and bones. Is that what you want for our son?"

"Well," the Masterji says. "It's her son . . . after what has happened . . ." The Masterji no longer seems capable of speaking in full sentences to Didi. He stutters and stumbles. There are moments when he appears to be speaking a foreign language, so hard is it to understand his words. "*Yo . . . Oohi . . . Tya . . .*" and he stops with a dazed expression. Vertical lines have appeared on the corners of his mouth that now make him look prematurely old. Even with his glasses on, he squints and makes faces when he reads. His blanket around him, he sits on his bed and tutors his students, but these days in a low, muted voice. Students still flock to him, but he makes mistakes, some of which his students catch.

"Once you declare someone your son," Didi tells the Masterji, "don't you then need to take care of him as if he's indeed your son?"

The Masterji smiles weakly. He knows that Apsara will put up a fight if he tries to snatch the boy away from her.

Tarun thinks that perhaps he should stay a night or two at Bangemudha just so he can see what his mother will do, whether that'll pull her out of her rut, and she'll come looking for him. He wonders how Amit will react if indeed Tarun starts living in Bangemudha. Sumit will be fine with it, even happy, for he likes Tarun, calls him "Tarun *da*," and when Amit is not present, follows Tarun around and obeys his instructions in play. But Amit's grudge against Tarun and Didi is growing. One Saturday Didi returned from the bazaar and handed Tarun and Sumit colorful sweet-smelling erasers, one each, which had images of the masked Betal. She told Amit that she ran out of money for a third one; besides, he was too big and could share Sumit's eraser. Amit snatched the eraser from Tarun's palm and said, "He can share with Sumit. I'll keep this." Didi's hand moved quickly through the air and landed on Amit's cheek, which turned red. He dropped the eraser to the floor, from where Sumit picked it up and handed it to Tarun. Sumit then offered his eraser to Amit, but he shoved away his younger brother's hand and stormed out of the house. Didi's thick fingers cupped Tarun's chin, and she asked, "Does my son like the eraser?" and Tarun nodded shyly. Not too long ago Mahesh Uncle had given Tarun a stationery box with a variety of pens and pencils, a ruler, and two erasers, but Didi's eraser was his favorite until it shriveled to a stub.

CHAPTER SEVEN

MAHESH UNCLE'S HOUSE is in Lazimpat, next to a hotel. The house has a gate with a guard who opens it and salutes you as the car glides in onto a paved driveway. The house, two stories with a marble façade, has a lawn big enough to play on. As Tarun enters the front door, he touches its wall, and Mahesh Uncle says, "It's from the quarry in Godavari."

Inside, there's a spacious living room with leather sofas, vases, paintings, and luxuriant rugs. The living room opens into a dining room, where there's a table large enough to accommodate ten people. There are three rooms upstairs, each with its own bed and furnishings, even though it's only Mahesh Uncle who lives on the upper floor. The old

servant Sanmaya sleeps in the small storage room next to
the kitchen. Mahesh Uncle says that he's asked her to move
to one of these empty rooms, but she refuses, says she likes
it down there, surrounded by sacks of rice and flour and
tins of dal and oil and tea.

Mahesh Uncle has never married, which is another reason that people say he has designs on Apsara. They say that
after all these years of living alone he has begun to yearn for
companionship. Those who are envious of his wealth and
contemptuous of Apsara say that he has found himself a
gold digger. Those who are sympathetic toward her say that
he wants to take undue advantage of a fallen woman. Those
who like both of them think that it's mutually beneficial:
she's saddled with a young son and needs a guardian, and
he needs a female companion for old age.

The large glass doors in the living room that Mahesh
Uncle refers to as "French windows" open to a sumptuous
garden enclosed within high walls. No noise from the street
encroaches; the walls also prevent obtrusive neighbors from
peeking in and coming to conclusions about your inner life.
There's a fountain against one of the walls. Water gurgles
from Lord Shiva's mouth and flows down in meandering
rivulets, as if he's spitting out River Ganga herself. The water
enters and exits other statues—Fat Buddha, Ganesh, Med-
itative Buddha, an owl, a dalmatian dog, a frog—moving
in and out of their bodies, forming small pools where lotus
flowers float. Mahesh Uncle says he designed the fountain
himself, and one of his foreigner friends built it. When it

was first built, Mahesh Uncle came here often, but now he's so busy with his work and his travels that when he comes home all he wants to do is take off his shoes and sit on the sofa with his legs pulled up and his newspaper on his lap. "Maybe you can take over this fountain, Tarun, and this garden," he says. He calls his garden a Japanese garden, and at first Tarun thinks he calls it Japanese because the builder, his friend, is from Japan. Then Mahesh Uncle explains that the garden is built in the Japanese style, with the fountain and the rocks placed in certain ways; although with the dalmatian and the Ganesh, the garden, he jokes, is more international than Japanese. His hand on Tarun's shoulder, he asks whether Tarun would like to be in charge of the garden, since Mahesh Uncle is getting old and needs someone responsible to make sure it works properly. Tarun nods shyly. "But, Tarun, how will you be the manager of this garden when you live in Kupondole? You'll have to travel here every day, maybe even twice a day, in order to water the plants and to make sure that the fountain flows well. I do have a gardener, but"—he lowers his voice to a whisper—"he's not reliable, and I need someone trustworthy to keep an eye on him. But how will you do it if you continue to live in Kupondole?" He addresses Apsara: "Why don't we make it simple and have you and Tarun move here? There are two rooms upstairs, sitting empty like unemployed workers. Our Tarun can have a separate room if he wants. And you can take that room"—he points to the window that overlooks the garden—"with a view of the garden. Sanmaya will take care of everything, the cooking, the laundry. Where's the harm in this?"

Apsara blushes red, as though Mahesh Uncle has made a marriage proposal. "We'll be a burden," she says. Her arms are crossed at her chest. She has half-heartedly combed her hair but she hasn't tied it properly because the wind is blowing it all over her face.

"What burden?" Mahesh Uncle says.

"I can't do it," she says.

Then Sanmaya comes into the garden to call them for dinner. She has wrinkled, pleated skin and teeth missing. But she has a big smile and bright eyes, and anyone Mahesh Uncle likes she likes, and anyone Mahesh Uncle dislikes she dislikes.

"*Dukh paryo timiharulai,*" she says inside when Mahesh Uncle is out of earshot. Apsara doesn't like words of pity and commiseration. But it's this very pride that makes her feel worse. She doesn't break down and cry. Tarun wishes she'd cry with Sanmaya when the old servant offers sympathy. He wishes his mother would admit that yes, we are suffering, I am suffering, and as a consequence my boy is suffering. He wishes she'd cry on Mahesh Uncle's wide shoulders, let him comfort her, perhaps even kiss her.

Mahesh Uncle is on the phone upstairs, so Sanmaya talks: "He thinks the world of you. I have never heard him speak as fondly about anyone as you two. He has been so alone for so long—it's really good to see him feel connected like this. People say about him, 'Oh, he is such a wealthy man living such a high life,' but these people are *murkhas*. What do they know about him? I have seen him in his loneliest state. I came to work for him when I was much younger, about twenty years ago. Did you know that he was already a successful businessman then? He is one of the most hardworking men I know. There is something in him, a drive, that most people don't have. Only very important people, like prime ministers and presidents, have that kind of drive.

"He started from scratch. He came to this city as a young boy, and at first he sold newspapers, then as he put himself through college he opened up a restaurant in Ranipokhari, when he was twenty. Twenty! The rest is history. Do you know that the finance minister has come to this house for dinner? And we've had parties where the who's who of this city have come. But he's never let his success go to his head. As big a man as he is, his heart is even bigger. Do you know how many struggling and suffering people he has helped? It will take me all day to count them. Yet he never asks anything in return, doesn't expect anything back. He doesn't even tell me when he has helped these people. I hear it from them, and they can't stop from singing his praises. I can tell you that when he wants you to come and live here, he has no ulterior motives. I know people are saying this and that, casting aspersions on his intentions, but I challenge these *murkhaharu* and *bekammaharu* to find me someone with a purer heart. I challenge them! In fact, I say that instead of talking behind his back, if they come and touch his feet, then the darkness in their own hearts will begin to evaporate."

Sanmaya goes on and on, but Tarun doesn't mind because he likes her leathery face and how the skin around her eyes turns into multiple folds when she smiles. Even when she's complaining and calling people *murkha*, her face is soft and open. Most important, she doesn't expect you to give her your undivided attention when she talks. She continues her monologue even when you're watching the birds in the garden or if you're staring at a painting or if you ask for a glass of water. So when Mahesh Uncle is on the phone, Sanmaya keeps on about what a great man he is, and Apsara, her gaze on the floor, is only half listening.

Tarun wonders if he is betraying her when he enjoys Didi's affection. His mother rarely asks about Tarun's Saturday visits to Bangemudha, but when Sanmaya briefly leaves the room, she asks him, "So what does the Masterji have to say when you visit? Anything?" She then asks about Amit and Sumit, trying to hide the bitterness in her voice, as though she really likes Didi's sons. Tarun tells her that they are fine and that he plays with them. He brings a neutral inflection into his voice, pretending that his playing with Amit and Sumit is the most natural thing in the world. His mother doesn't ask Tarun about Didi, but she says, "So you must have eaten delicious snacks in that house," and Tarun tells her, as indifferently as he can, "It was all right."

Tarun thinks how nice it would be if Didi also lived with them here. He imagines he and Didi sleeping in the same room upstairs, with Mahesh Uncle in the room that faces the main gate and his mother in the room from where she can view the fountain. But he knows this is foolish. Mahesh Uncle has gotten off the phone and entered the dining room now, and Sanmaya is serving the food on fine china plates and with polished cutlery.

Sanmaya is not as good a cook as Didi, but Tarun doesn't mind because he's enjoying the newness and the opulence of Mahesh Uncle's house: the chandeliers hanging from the ceiling, the lemon water in small bowls to dip their fingers in after they finish eating, Mahesh Uncle lighting his cigar. On the way back home in Mahesh Uncle's car, as they pass the Ratna Park area, Tarun glances toward the direction of Bangemudha. He thinks of Didi's *malpua*, and suddenly his mouth waters.

CHAPTER EIGHT

ONE EVENING APSARA doesn't come home. Tarun thinks that she has been delayed at work, although as the evening progresses this idea doesn't sound plausible, given that often she doesn't go to work in the first place. At ten o'clock, a neighbor knocks, asking for his mother. "She's working late today," Tarun tells her. The neighbor looks at him skeptically, then asks him whether he wants to wait for his mother in her flat instead of sitting here by himself. "I have homework to do," Tarun says.

All night long he waits in the dark. He thinks she is dead. Night noises come from surrounding houses and flats. An old woman coughs violently every hour or so. A baby mewls. He hears a rustle outside his door. It's not his mother's footsteps; he can tell. He pictures a rotund man with a snarling face, waiting for him to open the door. Tarun cries out for Didi, silently, and the rustling stops, only to start again some time later.

As soon as there's a tinge of light in the sky, he goes looking for his mother. After about an hour, he finds her asleep in a pavilion by the Bagmati shore. Her head is on the lap of a saffron-robed sadhu, whose eyes shine fiercely. Upon seeing Tarun, the sadhu puts his finger to his lips and says, "Shhh!"

"That's my mother," Tarun says, but he's scared of the sadhu's unruly beard and his gleaming eyes. The man's long, blackened fingers stroke her forehead and smooth her wrinkles. Tarun leaves the pavilion, bewildered about what he should do. He wanders along the Bagmati shore, hoping he won't run into one of his river friends—they live somewhere around here, don't they? He considers going to Bangemudha and telling Didi and his father about what has happened, but he doesn't want to cast his mother in any more of a negative light. Then he is in the Tripureswor area, and as the streets become filled with the hazy morning light, he finds a store with a phone and calls Mahesh Uncle, who has to be roused from his sleep. He tells the boy to stay where he is, and in about half an hour he arrives, driving his car.

She has already left the sadhu's side, and Tarun and Mahesh Uncle go to the flat, where she's sitting by the window, whimpering, calling out Tarun's name. "*Kahan harayeko*, Apsara?" Mahesh Uncle asks. "The boy has been worried sick." But her tear-streaked face is fixed on Tarun, and she continues to mumble his name. She looks like a street crazy who curses invisible people. Mahesh Uncle asks the boy to pack everything, and he, too, stuffs clothes and knickknacks into empty suitcases and bags, while Apsara watches. Mahesh Uncle says, "I'll send the driver later to pick up the rest of your belongings." When Mahesh Uncle asks her to stand, she refuses, saying she's not going anywhere. Mahesh Uncle crouches in front of her and uses a velvety voice to *fakau fulau* her, telling her that it's a temporary solution meant more for Tarun than for her. The boy shouldn't have to go through what he went through seeing her in the pavilion with the sadhu, Mahesh Uncle tells her. Her eyes open wide in shame; she hadn't known until then that Tarun had seen her on the sadhu's lap. She covers her face with her palm.

The Masterji is not happy about the move. "Who is this man?" he asks. He has known about Mahesh Uncle for a while now, how he is fond of Tarun and Apsara. A separate room for each of them? Yes, Tarun has a room to himself, with a proper bed, not bedding spread on the floor. There's a bedside table on which Sanmaya puts a jug of water in case he gets thirsty during the night. Before he sleeps she brings him a warm glass of milk to drink and sits with him with that toothless smile of hers as he holds the glass with both palms and drinks. She leaves only after the boy has finished the milk and handed the glass to her. "*Ramrari sutnu, la?*" she says as she shuts the door behind her.

Next door is Mahesh Uncle, and Tarun can hear him on the phone. Words such as "commission," "contract," and "discount" and "percent" have become familiar to Tarun by now because Mahesh Uncle uses them quite a bit. Just hearing his voice makes Tarun feel good.

Mahesh Uncle's intentions are not good, the Masterji is implying, but he's looking at Didi to judge whether she approves of what he's just said so he can carry his thoughts further and end them in some type of action, something like marching over to Lazimpat and wrenching the boy away from Mahesh Uncle. But Didi doesn't engage her husband; she gets up and walks into the kitchen. Sumit is busy smiling into a comic book. Amit is in the corner watching Tarun and Didi. These days he watches the two quite a bit. Tarun follows Didi into the kitchen. She doesn't turn to him, but her voice is pleasing enough when she asks him, "And what would my son like to eat?"

"French toast," he says. He wishes she'd turn to him and embrace him. But she is busy rinsing dishes at the sink. "*Pauroti ta chha tara anda chaina.* Amit, run to the store and bring an egg for your brother."

Amit doesn't move. Didi raises her voice. "Didn't you hear? I need an egg to make French toast for your brother." She says *frentos* in her village woman's pronunciation. She learned how to make it after she came to know that Apsara made it regularly for him. Didi's French toast is thicker, more succulent than his mother's.

Amit stands and leans against the wall, his arms crossed. "Why only for him? Why not Sumit and me also?"

"Didn't you and Sumit have a boiled egg each this morning? And now your brother, who visits once a week, wants some French toast, you get huffy?"

"But we only had a boiled egg, not French toast. We'd also like French toast. We're also hungry."

"Okay, I can't win with you. Get three eggs then."

Amit mutters and leaves. Didi turns to Tarun and says, "Now that you've moved to a big man's house, you're going to forget about us all, aren't you? You're going to forget about me."

He moves to her and embraces her. In her left hand she has a towel and in her right a plate, and she doesn't put them down, like she usually does, so she can hug him. His face is buried in her stomach; he's trying not to show that he's teary eyed. He looks up to see that the Masterji is watching them and that Sumit is happy with something he sees in his comic book. Tarun feels a dark twisting inside his stomach: Didi is withholding her affection. She is not going to hug or embrace him nor acknowledge his tears. He's on his own now. Amit enters with the eggs in his hands, and upon seeing Tarun with his arms around his mother, he rolls his eyes in exasperation. "One minute I'm away," he says. He makes the gesture of hurling the eggs toward them, one by one. Didi doesn't see him, but the Masterji does, and Tarun observes him shaking his head at Amit.

Didi serves French toast to the three boys, but she is grim, and Tarun anxiously searches her face to see if she'll smile at him, ruffle his hair, caress him, call him "my son" in a voice meant only for him, a voice that emerges from the depths of her throat and enters his ears, then goes down and vibrates in his belly, where it stays, warm and alive, for days. Without it today his stomach is already hollow. The French toast tastes dry and leathery. After several unpleasant bites, he says, "*Bathroom janu paryo,*" and he runs to the toilet. He retches. As he sits on his haunches on the toilet, small globules of blood drip down from his anus and scatter on the porcelain. He grunts, tears falling, and after a few more drops the bleeding stops. I'll go to her and tell her about the blood, he thinks, but then he pictures her face, the eyes that are impassive, unresponsive, and he knows that if she doesn't show concern he won't be able to take it. So after he washes himself and gets out of the bathroom, he heads straight for the door.

"*Kahaan jaana la?*" his father asks.

"I'm not feeling well. I'm going to go home."

"Your new home, *da?*" Sumit asks. "When are you going to invite us?"

Amit punches him on the shoulder.

Didi is watching him, but she's not smiling.

"What about your French toast?" the Masterji asks.

"My stomach is hurting."

He wants Didi to come to him, ask him solicitously where it hurts, then take him to bed and gently knead his stomach. But she doesn't.

CHAPTER NINE

TARUN CAN'T SLEEP. The newness of Mahesh Uncle's house, which excited him at first, now makes him feel like a stranger. His mother is next door, with her rustling and her mumbling. There are days when she sleeps all afternoon and is up throughout the night. One night he awakens and goes downstairs, where he finds her in the living room, lying on the floor with her arms and legs stretched out. The death pose, she says. *Shavasana.* She asks him to lie down with her. Another night she comes to his room just as he is about to sleep and strokes his forehead and asks him how things are at school. Before he can answer, she begins talking about a picnic she went on when she was a young girl.

He is used to her erratic ways by now, and he has come

to accept that this is his lot. At school sometimes a new friend will ask him, "So, is it true that your mother has lost her mind?" and he answers tactfully, "She has a problem or two." He's calm about his mother, which makes his friends calm about him and his mother. His friends flock around him—he is well loved. Tarun also gets good report cards. He's the type that the teachers call on, for he provides cogent, well-considered answers. The teachers also like the calmness he exudes. "Tarun, *gharma saab thik chha?*" they ask, putting their arms around him. "Your mother is fine?"

But now Tarun is so troubled by Didi's withholding of affection that he can't pay attention in school. When the teachers call on him, he gropes for answers. Two of his friends ask him whether things are all right with his mother—it doesn't occur to them that things might not be all right with his stepmother. They all know that every Saturday he goes to Bangemudha to spend time with his father and his village family. They know that the older of the stepbrothers is a bully. They know that the stepmother loves Tarun.

One day after school he gets off the bus at Ranipokhari instead of Lazimpat. He walks into Asan and moves through the lanes that surround the Bangemudha house, hoping he won't bump into Amit or Sumit, either of whom could be nearby running errands or hanging out with friends. They are sure to ask him what he's doing in Bangemudha on a school day. Amit is sure to jab him on the shoulder and say, "What's up with you? *Ta muji randiko chhorako yahaan yetibela ke kaam?* Isn't it enough that you show us your ugly face once a week?" And he might even kick Tarun, and what answer will Tarun give? That he is here to check on Didi to see if she is still unhappy with him? Tarun will laugh his head off then, call him a namby-pamby.

Tarun circles and circles the area but doesn't dare to move into the lane where the house is located. He doesn't run into Amit or Sumit, although he does come across a couple of the neighborhood boys he knows through Amit. When darkness begins to fall, Tarun moves closer to the lane, and when it's completely dark he gathers the nerve to walk by the house. There's light in the kitchen window. He spots Didi, part of her head, shoulders, her side profile. She is cooking, her attention on the stove. To his left, through the living room window, he sees a figure move toward the kitchen—Amit—and sharp words are exchanged between him and Didi. A pressure cooker hisses. Didi turns her attention back to the stove again. She lifts her head as if she's sensed something.

Tarun retreats into the shadows of the house across the street. Didi leans sideways toward the window and peers out, her eyes devouring the darkness. *"Kina andhyaroma lukira?"* A voice startles Tarun. It's the old man who does odd jobs in the Bangemudha house. He smells of alcohol. "Oh, I see, you're playing hide-and-seek with your brothers." The man smiles drunkenly. Didi can see the man because he's under the streetlamp. After the man leaves, Didi lingers at the window, her eyes boring into the spot where Tarun is flattened against the wall. Then she returns to her cooking.

At school Tarun's eyes tear up for no reason, even when he's not thinking about Didi. He can no longer answer questions from his teachers. He sounds almost like his father: "Um . . . aah . . . *tyo . . . yo . . . yahan.*" His classmates laugh. At home he answers in monosyllables to Sanmaya and Mahesh Uncle. These days Apsara mostly stays cooped up inside her room. Sanmaya has to take her food on a tray upstairs and sometimes leave it outside her door, like in a hotel. Some days Apsara pulls the tray into her room, and some days it sits outside, the food turning stale. Every now and then Tarun picks up the tray from outside the door and carries it into her room. At other times, when it strikes her fancy, she opens the door. One time she opened the door and talked to him rapidly about something she did with her aunt when she was a child, something about the sewing of leaves to make plates for a festival.

Today as he takes the tray into her room, she launches into a description of her childhood picnic, how it was on a hill with a breathtaking view of the mountains. "The mountains looked gorgeous enough to be swallowed," she said. Sanmaya must have persuaded her to take a bath recently because her hair is combed and oiled. "How do you swallow mountains, Ma?" the boy asks. She laughs. She names her friends who were there: Sarita, Sunita, Bonita, this ta, that ta. The food: *pulao, khasi ko masu, kerau ko achar, koreko mula,* roasted corn.

"Let's have that picnic right here," Tarun says, and she nods. "*Aaan garnus,*" he commands, then inserts his fingers full of rice and dal and *tarkari* into her open mouth. There's someone standing at the door. Mahesh Uncle. He's back home early today. "Fabulous," he says.

"We're having a picnic," Apsara says, then thinks of something and stops eating. Mahesh Uncle leaves, and it takes the boy a while to coax her back to the picnic.

Tarun doesn't go to Bangemudha for a week, then two. Finally after skipping two Saturdays, he goes. When he opens the door and enters, there's no one in the house. Normally his father would be on the bed; Amit and Sumit would be around somewhere, Amit sulking, Sumit smiling. But today there's an air of stillness. Somehow the noises of the street have also become muted. Tarun stands quietly by the door.

Didi emerges from the kitchen. She looks younger, perhaps because of the hair cascading on her shoulders—he's never seen her hair down before—but also because, Tarun realizes with a start, her lips are red. She has lipstick on. And her eyes look darker because she has put kohl around them. The way she's wearing her dhoti, it looks different, not loose but tightly wrapped around her hips. The boy becomes transfixed. She stops a few feet away from him. "You finally remembered me."

Tarun's throat is so tight that he doesn't know what sound will leap out if he speaks.

"So, how does it feel to abandon your mother like this?"

Tarun is crying now.

"And what made you remember me today?"

Tarun is shaking his head, blubbering. He has no excuse. It is all his fault.

"And what do you want from me today?" she asks.

Her words pierce him, and he crumples to the ground, on his knees, his hands clasped together in front of his chest. "Please, Didi."

She comes close to him and stands a few inches away. She's breathing heavily. "Stand up," she says. He does. He's afraid of meeting her eyes, but he can't help himself, so he lifts his gaze. Her eyes are big and shiny and filled with something that seems to want to swallow him.

Her fingers reach out and grab his chin, rougher than usual. "Let me see this man's face." She inspects it, and when he makes a gesture to move closer to her, she steps back a few inches and says, "No, you can't touch me."

His eyes fill up again.

"If you want to touch me," she says, "you have to prove yourself again."

He lets her stroke his face, rub her hand behind his ears. The loose end of her dhoti falls from her chest, exposing a brightly patterned blouse—he's never seen her in that blouse either. She makes no attempt to gather the dhoti end and cover herself again: he can see the heave of her chest with each breath. "My son," she says as her finger slides across his lips. "You have no idea how much your mother missed you."

"Where are the others?"

"I sent them away so it'll only be you and me."

"Where did they go?"

"To the village, for a week. Your father needs to take care of some matter regarding the house."

"What about Amit's and Sumit's school?"

"One week isn't going to hurt them. Are you hungry?"

He nods.

"What would you like to eat? Whatever my son wants to eat today, I'll cook for him."

"I want to eat some *kheer*."

"Then I'll cook some *kheer*."

She asks him to stay in the kitchen with her as she cooks. She's tucked her dhoti end into her waist so her breasts bounce as she moves. His eyes become fixed on them, and she smiles at him. Her body still hasn't welcomed him to hers. But every now and then her hand reaches out to touch his face—his eyes, his cheeks, his lips—and his neck and shoulders; once, her hand rubs his chest as she cooks.

When he gazes at her face, the red lipstick makes him think this is what his mother must have looked like when she was younger, except, of course, his mother was prettier. Yet when Tarun looks at Didi now, he doesn't think she's ugly. He's come to like the fleshiness of her cheeks, the chubby nose, the black spots on her face. Besides the red lipstick, she has also applied some powder to her cheeks, because there's a sheen to them.

When the *kheer* is ready, she ladles some on a plate and takes it to the bed, where they both sit. When he tries to scoot closer to her, she says, "You're still not allowed to touch me, but I'll feed you." And she lovingly feeds him, watches him chew and swallow the kheer. "*Mitho chha?*" she asks several times and, his mouth full, he nods. At one point he asks her if she's going to eat, and she says her hunger is satiated by just looking at him. There's something odd about the way her voice is coming from a different place inside her. After he finishes a second helping of the *kheer*, he lets out a loud burp, and she laughs. "I guess you don't want any more?" she asks.

He shakes his head. "Then why don't you lie down?" she says. He's eaten so much that he is feeling drowsy, so he lies down on the bed, the bed where the Masterji sleeps at night. Since she came to Bangemudha, Didi hasn't slept on the same bed with the Masterji; she sleeps by herself in a corner.

He wonders if Amit and Sumit are enjoying the village. Did they really want to go? He's heard Amit say a few times that he wasn't going to return to that backward hole even if someone dragged him there in chains, and Sumit had smiled and said, "Yes, a backward hole." Did they go willingly, or did Didi force them? He suspects the latter. As he begins to doze, he is aware that Didi is closing the curtains to the windows that overlook the street. Why is she doing that? he wonders, but he's too sleepy to wonder more. Then she slides next to him, and he can smell her—she's put on some kind of perfume!—and her breasts press against him. Her hands begin to roam all over his body, and she calls his name over and over in endearment.

A week later when the Masterji returns to the city with Amit and Sumit, there's a smell in the house he can't identify. "What's this smell? *Yo . . . tyo . . . ?* What is it?" The Masterji goes around sniffing but can't place the smell. Amit thinks something is odd about his mother, something off. She appears to have become younger, her skin smoother; she seems to have become . . . prettier. How is that possible? She must have taken a lover—this realization jolts him, and he looks for clues to validate the presence of another man: cigarette butts around the house, a slip of paper with an unknown handwriting, perhaps a shaving blade left in the bathroom. There's nothing. When Tarun comes to visit the following Saturday, Amit finds him on the front lawn and punches him harder than ever before. Tarun kneels and gasps in pain, and Didi flies out and strikes Amit on the face with such force that he's sent reeling across the yard. "If you touch your brother again," she says, "I will kill you."

She takes Tarun by his shoulder and leads him in, where she has him open his shirt. She rubs some Vicks at the point of contact, saying she hopes the bastard hasn't broken her beautiful son's shoulder bone. Poor baby, Amit thinks, watching his mother rub Vicks with the tips of two fingers and blow a soft gentle breath on them. The way his mother's fingers clasp Tarun's naked shoulder, and the smell of Vicks, which his mother applies liberally, take Amit back to the uneasiness he'd experienced after returning from the village. His mind tries, vaguely, to connect the two feelings, the then-feeling and the now-feeling, but the two mingle and become diffused and confusing. "My beautiful son," his mother is whispering to Tarun.

CHAPTER TEN

Every few weeks there's an opportunity for Tarun to be alone with Didi. Somehow the other members of the house are away, and when he reaches Bangemudha, he finds the house quiet. Soon after he enters, she pulls the curtains and bolts the door, and suddenly the outside world is shut off. "Come here, sweet son," Didi says to him. She sits on the chair by the door, and he goes to her with dread and excitement in his throat. When he nears her, he can feel heat coming off her body. Her eyes become slightly glazed, and her chest moves up and down as though she's begun panting inside. When he is inches from her, she reaches out to explore him. Her hands at first move rapidly up and down his body, an initial survey of the landscape. He's ticklish and laughs, but she's not laughing. She begins with the chest, where she gently rubs her palm in a circular motion. Soft, moaning breaths are coming out of her parted lips. Some days she calls him by his name, "Taruuuun, Taruuuun." He's mesmerized by her voice, which sounds like a small animal trapped in the thicket of the jungle. Her fingers move up toward his face. They linger for a long time on his lips. "My sweet boy. Is there anyone more beautiful in this world? Is there anyone who loves his Didi more?" She's not seeking answers to these questions, for in the next second he's in her arms, and she's kissing him on his lips, first with great tenderness, then strongly. A hand moves down to his privacy. Without him wanting to, he starts becoming hard, and he recalls a Bangemudha kid saying "*lando*" as he emphatically grabbed his crotch. *Lando*, Tarun thinks, and he becomes even harder. "Becoming bigger," Didi whispers. She deep kisses him, her tongue darting in and out of his mouth, her lips sucking his tongue. Her hand is softly massaging his privacy. He's confused and a bit scared and wants to move away, yet it also feels good.

At home, he avoids his mother. He doesn't have to try too hard because she's often in her own world. Sometimes when he returns home, he finds her on the lawn. Sanmaya has helped her bathe, oiled her hair, and put her out in the sun. He doesn't meet her eyes. She stares at him as he goes into the house. He runs up to his room and lies in bed, breathing heavily, his eyes closed. He hates himself.

On some days after Didi is finished with him, his lips are

sore and swollen. Amit notices and asks him why. Tarun doesn't answer and looks down. Amit calls him a sissy, says his lips look like those of a girl's *puti*. He comes closer to Tarun, says, "Do you know who has a smelly *puti*? Your mother." Amit nods sagaciously. "That's what my father smelled, but he liked it." A pause. "That's how you were born."

Back in Lazimpat Tarun fingers his swollen lips. Sanmaya thinks he got into a fight, so she fusses over him. He brushes her hand away. In his room he stares at his lips in the mirror, whispers, "*Puti.*" After making sure the door is locked, he takes off all his clothes. He imagines Didi's hands over his body, and his *lando* stiffens. He watches it rise. It's pencil thin, but it has a throb of its own. He twists his body this way and that, as though looking for an elusive scar. Beautiful boy, he mouths to his reflection. He wonders what Didi finds beautiful about him, what others do. His body is scrawny, and lately he thinks his face is like a girl's. He is certain that his lips, even when they aren't swollen, look like *puti*. He doesn't know what a *puti* looks like. One time a boy at school brought a tattered book with photos of naked women, but the photos were black and white and grainy, and one photo was a close-up of a *puti* with the caption VULVA in English underneath. But all it resembled was a cave with some hair hanging from it. Still, it was ugly, and he thinks his face looks like the vulva.

Every time he returns home after spending private time with Didi, he becomes despondent for a day or two. He loses his appetite, and when Mahesh Uncle and Sanmaya talk to him, he barely responds. "Why so glum today?" Sanmaya remarks. Mahesh Uncle asks whether Amit bullied him again today. Tarun shakes his head no. Mahesh Uncle has heard about Amit's aggression, not from Tarun but from Sanmaya after Tarun told her about Amit locking him in the outside shed in Bangemudha for nearly an hour one afternoon. "Tell me if he does anything like that again," Mahesh Uncle had said then. "Maybe you need to stop going to Bangemudha." But if Tarun stopped going to Bangemudha, Didi would be distressed, so he's been keeping mum about Amit's bullying.

Amit confronts him on the side of the house, the narrow strip enclosed by a wall that separates the neighbor's house. Sumit is somewhere else. "Eh, *randi ko chhora,*" he says, grabbing Tarun by the collar. "*Muji,* you come here on Saturdays when we're not here, don't you?"

Tarun nods.

"Why?"

He has no answer for Amit, who briefly lets go of Tarun's collar, slaps him, then grabs the collar again with the same hand. The smoothness of the gesture indicates it's copied from a movie and practiced. "Tell me," Amit says. "What do you come here for?" He's speaking in a loud, urgent whisper. They are underneath the window of the living room, and the Masterji is inside, sitting cross-legged on the bed poring over a book. Didi is most likely inside, too.

Didi and the Masterji rarely speak to each other; rather, it's Didi who rarely speaks to the Masterji, who generally avoids Didi's eyes. But the Masterji, even if he knew Amit was strong-arming Tarun, would not have gotten up from his seat to stop it; he'd have looked on helplessly or offered a mild rebuke to Amit, who'd have merely sneered at his father.

"*Ta machikney*, you think you can come here and do whatever you want?" Amit grabs Tarun's collar tighter, knuckles pressing against Tarun's throat. He smells of *khaini*; his right cheek has the small bulge of the tobacco ensconced there. Sumit has informed Tarun that his brother is already smoking ganja with the neighborhood boys.

Amit's voice is now a soft whisper. "She's sucking your *lando*, isn't she, my mother?"

Fear grips Tarun, and reflexively he drives his knee into Amit's groin, feeling something crunch against his knee bone. Holding his crotch, Amit collapses to the ground, his face contorted in pain. Just then Didi and Sumit emerge from the front of the house. She observes Amit with distaste, then crouches in front of Tarun and checks his face for damages. She brushes her thumb against his lips, then takes him inside. Sumit attends to his brother.

Tarun worries about Amit telling everyone about him and Didi, or seeking revenge, but strangely, Amit seems to have acquired a new respect for Tarun. On the next visit, Amit even shows him his swollen testicles. Now he's less aggressive toward him. He still calls Tarun names, and sometimes he mouths them across the room when Didi's back is turned, but now there's an undercurrent of jocularity to it, as though the two share an inside joke. He never mentions his suspicion about Didi and Tarun again, but once or twice when Didi demonstrates affection toward Tarun, Amit is in the background, making kissing gestures, and once, he lewdly grabs his crotch. When Tarun runs into Amit with his friends on street corners, Amit warns them, "If any of you lay a finger on him, you'll find your arms and legs broken." He puts his arm around Tarun. "This brother of mine is a *chhupe rustam*. He looks like a pretty girl, but he's got many tricks up his sleeve."

When Tarun turns twelve he ejaculates as Didi is fondling him over his trousers. His crotch becomes wet. He is ashamed and stands stiffly, as though called to attention at a Boy Scout march. "I was wondering when this would happen," Didi says. "All this means is that you've become a big boy now. But we'll need to get you cleaned up. Come, take off your clothes." He covers his crotch with his palms. She looks at him questioningly. "What's the matter, love?" He shakes his head. "Is my beautiful boy shy? Is he ashamed about what his mother will see?" She's happy at the idea of him shy about revealing himself to her. "But we'll need to get you washed up before the others come. You don't want them to find out, do you? You don't want Amit to know, do you?" She rubs her index finger over the wet spot on his trousers, then brings it up to her nose to sniff. "A big boy that you are now, you can't let other people see these things. It's okay if I see it, I'm your mother. But it has to remain our secret, do you understand?"

He nods.

"Come, let's take off your clothes."

He allows her to take off his shirt, then his pants. He has on white underwear. She cups his crotch with her palm and says, "Oh, look, how big the spot is on your *kattu*." She pulls down his underwear and inspects his penis. There is a globule of semen on its tip, like creamy dew. She picks up the globule with her fingertip and tastes it with her tongue.

In the bathroom she washes him. The water is cold. He shivers. She's business-like now, and her able hands soap him all over. He whimpers when the soap stings his eyes; she flicks away the soapsuds from around them. She briskly rubs him under his armpits, then the crack in his buttocks and his balls and his penis. "How can she call herself a mother?" Didi grumbles. "She ought to have died soon after giving birth to you so I'd have you all to myself." She pours water over him to wash away the soap. "Soon, I'll make my son some *chouchou* soup so he'll be warm and cozy." She fetches a towel and rubs him until warmth spreads through his muscles and skin. She leads him to the living room and grabs a pair of Amit's pants and puts them on him. They're slightly big for him, so she has to fold the bottom as well as the waist. She has him sit on the bed with a thick blanket around him, like his father, then she goes to the kitchen.

Tarun thinks that somehow Mahesh Uncle and his mother are going to discover that he's ejaculated. He thinks it'll be obvious on his face, a telltale sign that all adults know. And once they learn this truth, then the truth about him and Didi will also be forced out into the open. So for a couple of days he avoids everyone in Lazimpat. Even when he's talking to Mahesh Uncle or Sanmaya, he turns his face away. But Mahesh Uncle is especially busy with his work and doesn't dwell upon Tarun's behavior. And Sanmaya is too busy with her own talk; besides, she doesn't see too well. And his mother? Whenever she gets a chance she escapes Lazimpat and fitfully walks through the city. Mostly, her eyes are fixed on the pavement, but even when she lifts her head, she doesn't appear conscious of much, except not running into traffic. At times her lips move silently; at times words fly out, but no one understands what she's saying. She trudges in her worn house dhoti, her hair uncombed, dragging her slippers. Street urchins follow her, make faces, calling her names to taunt her. Drunk and perverted men block her way, making suggestions, for she still has the air of a former beauty. She doesn't venture into the city center, toward Bangemudha; it's as though she has forgotten that part of her life.

By the time he is fourteen, Tarun is somewhat of a loner. He has friends, but he prefers his own company. He comes up with excuses not to spend time with friends. "I have things to do at home," he tells them. He uses his mother as an excuse. "Today, my mother is in an especially bad state," he says when he's asked to join them for an outing or for a movie or just to relax on someone's roof listening to music and smoking a cigarette or two. He is well liked, for he is mild mannered and considerate, but over time his friends have grown weary of how much persuasion he needs before he agrees to their company. He's acquired a reputation as a lone wolf. When he does get together with them, he ends up faking a headache to leave early so he can then be alone with his own thoughts or go home and listen to music in the quietude of his own room. Or masturbate. When he masturbates he tries hard to think of girls, but in the end it's Didi he thinks of and comes, quickly and without fuss.

"Think of pretty chicks," Amit had said when he'd demonstrated for Tarun and Sumit and a handful of neighborhood boys how to masturbate. They were in a patch of bamboo grove near their house, and Amit had dropped his shorts and taken out his penis, which was long and twisted at the top. "See this beautiful creature?" he'd said, stroking it and watching it grow. "This *bhai* will happily serve many maidens for years." He petted it, and it slowly raised its head like an animal aroused from sleep. "*Dai,*" cautioned Sumit, but he was smiling as usual. "And so this is how you masturbate," he said, and his hand moved at first leisurely, then rapidly. "It helps if you think of pretty chicks." He mentioned the names of a girl or two they all knew. He told his rapt audience that he was concentrating on one of those girls, then he shuddered and came.

But Tarun gets anxious with pretty girls. He thinks they won't find him manly enough. He pictures pretty girls laughing at him, making fun of his penis, which is smaller than Amit's. It's slightly larger than Sumit's—he'd taken a glance when they'd peed together into the bushes—but that hardly seems like a consolation. More important, no matter what its size, he feels like he has a child's penis and that pretty girls will simply laugh him away. He is convinced that they call him a sissy behind his back. He pictures them saying to one another, *Who would want to be with him? He's a dirty little boy.* Deep inside, he knows that girls don't talk about him that way. If anything, he's aware of how the eyes of the girls linger on him. He's heard whispers of "handsome" and "good-looking," but he's convinced that after a short conversation with him they will realize what a pansy and how unmanly he is, and his good looks won't matter. Once they discover that he's not worth their time, they'll gravitate toward someone like Amit. Yes, Tarun can see how these girls would throw Amit admiring glances. Amit has a perpetually sneering expression, and he leers at girls. One time he made a fornicating gesture with his hands at a girl who was sitting at her window near Bangemudha, a girl rumored to be loose. This happened toward early evening when people were about. Tarun was mortified, but the girl only preened and smiled and left the window. Tarun thought about that girl for many days. It was manly, that gesture. The girl had liked it. Girls liked such displays of manliness. He practiced the gesture in

front of the mirror: the left index finger and thumb forming a tight hole, and the right index finger pumping it like
a piston. But when Tarun did it, it looked like a timid boy
playing with his fingers, like girls play with dolls.

CHAPTER ELEVEN

SILENTLY THEY MOVE toward each other and embrace. He is as tall as she is, yet in that moment he is the child who used to follow her around the house, cling to her dhoti, and eat her food.

She smothers his lips with hers. She has lipstick on. "My beautiful son," she says. She cries, "I haven't feasted my eyes on you for days." She plants kisses all over his face, his neck. Her hand gently rubs his crotch. From the corner of his eyes, he notices that the curtains on the window facing the street aren't closed, and with one hand he reaches over to close them, but she clasps him tightly and says, "Let them be. It doesn't matter." Still, his fingers strain and pull them shut. In the back of his mind, he thinks Amit can walk in on them—these days Amit makes sudden, brief appearances to eat, then leaves—and Tarun stretches his neck to look at the door, which is latched shut.

She runs her hand over his body hungrily, overzealously, as though she'll not get another opportunity like this. They shuffle toward the bed, where, as soon as they lie down, she reaches inside his pants and touches him. He ejaculates instantly in her hand. Her wet hand still inside his pants, she smiles, like she smiles when he gulps down her food and lets out a burp. They lie together like this for a few minutes. She says she'll clean him up before others come, and he says he'll do it himself. Let me do it, Son, she says. He blushes, shakes his head. You love your Didi, don't you? she asks. He nods. You love me more than you love your mother? she asks slyly. He's silent, then he says, I love you more than my mother. She closes her eyes and takes a long breath, gratified. I'm your real mother, am I not, even though I'm ugly? Please say yes, *chora*. He's quiet again, then he says, Yes, you are my real mother. Her eyes are still closed; her lips are quivering.

Later, as he's cleaning himself in the bathroom, he hears Sumit and his father enter. "The doctor said that it's mild bronchitis, but that it could become severe," Sumit explains. The Masterji coughs violently. When Tarun emerges from the bathroom, he has his shirt out, covering the wet patch on his crotch. Didi hasn't yet wiped off her lipstick. As Sumit leads his father to the bed, the Masterji repeatedly glances at Didi's face, then he studies Tarun, and something shifts in his eyes. His nose gives an involuntary twitch: the smell in the room has hit his nostrils. The Masterji crawls into bed. Didi stands over him next to the bed and says, "Poor soul. I'll make some soup for you. You'll feel better."

One day Apsara happens to be in Naxal, on the street where she grew up. It's hard to tell whether she's cognizant of her old neighborhood, for her face is devoid of any expression. Her mother, Tarun's grandmother, spots her from the window. With uncharacteristic compassion, her mother rushes down and goes to her. Caressing her daughter's cheek in the middle of the street—neighbors are watching; they know who Apsara is, her history—Tarun's grandmother says, "Look what has become of you." But one gets the feeling that it's mostly for show, for she's aware that some could criticize her for being a heartless mother. "Won't you come inside?" she says. "Won't you stay for a while with your old mother? Look how my heart has been torn to pieces seeing you like this." Tarun's uncle has already married and moved to a new place. Apsara hasn't set foot inside this house since that fateful day when she took Tarun with her to Kupondole. The kitchen has been remodeled, so there is a shiny new counter and an island in the middle, a place "where I can chop carrots and cauliflower with ease," Apsara's mother informs her daughter. Apsara takes everything in. Nothing about her childhood home evokes anything anymore. There are old photographs on the wall of the living room. She with her brother taken at a portrait studio, she in cowboy attire, and her brother dressed as an American Indian. A photo of her during her college days. She is alone in that photograph, her eager face thrust at the camera. Her mother catches her observing her photo and weeps. "*Chhori, chhori*, what happened? Look at you in that photo! And look at you now." She runs her hand through her daughter's stringy hair; she fingers her daughter's worn-out dhoti. But in the end, nothing comes out of this visit. Apsara doesn't return to her maternal home, and her mother doesn't make overtures to bring her daughter and her grandson back into her life.

Didi allows him to pet her breasts now. She opens her blouse and her bra, and he rubs and fondles her nipples. Her nipples are dark, resembling the black spots on her face. He also clumsily sucks on them, but they give off an odor, like the smell of damp clothes. Yet he thinks they are beautiful. She strokes the back of his head and encourages him as he sucks on them. She doesn't appear aroused, merely pleased, and sometimes overwhelmed with emotion. When he looks up from her breasts, she says, "You have to promise you won't ever leave me."

He, too, is affected by her emotions, and he can barely get his words out. "I'll never leave you, Didi."

"Do you promise?"

"I promise." And he moves up to her face and kisses her deeply and passionately on the mouth. He feels like a man kissing a woman. "I'll take care of you, don't worry," he says. Even his voice becomes rougher, like Amit's, and he kisses her a bit forcefully. She's pleasantly surprised, for she says, "How strong you're becoming." He feels powerful and kisses her more. It occurs to him that no boy his age, not even Amit, has access to a full-grown woman like this. The other boys are only talk and no action, and here he is, sucking on a real woman's breasts.

He is hard, and Didi's fingers are inside his underwear, stroking. "My son has become really big now." At her words he spurts all over her hand.

"It's so nice, just you and me," Didi says. "No one in this world has a clue about the deep love you and I have for each other. Your father, well, I'm sure he's dying of jealousy." She laughs softly. "This jealous world will try to tear us apart, Tarun, do you understand? You won't let it happen, will you, Son? Will you let anyone come between us?"

"I won't let anyone come between us."

"I knew it," she says, and kisses him with much feeling.

It's true: he can't imagine not being with Didi. What would he do? Where would he go? He'd be so alone in this world.

He hasn't told Didi about his struggle with pretty girls. Not too long after Amit used the fornicating gesture at the girl, Tarun passed by her house and saw her at her window. His heart hammering, he lifted his arms and performed the obscene gesture. She stared, then—her face contorted—spat at him. Her spit missed him, but he got some sprinkles. Her response devastated him, depleted him. It was a confirmation that pretty girls—this one isn't even that pretty, more "sexy," as Amit informed the boys—sense that something is wrong with him, that he is weak and vulgar. Maybe this girl knows about him and Didi? But how is that possible? How can this girl who lives fifteen houses away have the knowledge of what goes on behind the white curtains in the Bangemudha house?

But whenever he tells Didi about his thoughts on girls, she says, "All these girls are not worth your time. These *sahariya* types. They'll stab you in the back the first chance they get. They don't have any morals, just like your mother. Look at how she so unabashedly fornicated with your father. The only good thing she did was bring you into this world." She says this when they're lying together in the Masterji's bed. Tarun is pressed against her, his head resting on the crook of her arm. She is always fully clothed during these hours of intimacy. Even when she gives him her breasts she doesn't remove her bra or her blouse, only opens her clothing halfway so he can reach them. She takes off his clothes for him, usually commenting on how she never gets enough of looking at him, kissing him on the shoulder, on the neck, on his ears, and on his mouth. She leaves his underwear on because she likes looking at his bulge.

Sometimes her hand stays down there, gently massaging. He knows that at any moment he'll come in her hand. But she also stops massaging for a minute or so to elongate his pleasure, and hers. There are days when she makes him come twice.

"It's as though God forced your mother to give birth to you as a gift for me," she says. "For some reason you were not supposed to come out of my womb, although by all means you should have. Maybe God screwed up." She laughs. "It doesn't matter. By all accounts you're my baby. You came from here." She takes his hand and places it on her stomach. She covers his hand with her big hands and says, "This is where you came out of. I don't care what that Apsara Thapa says, or your weakling of a father says, I don't care what *anyone* says." She says "anyone" with much venom. "You were in here for nine months, in the year between Amit and Sumit. I remember your kicks. I remember thinking then that once you were born people would be amazed that such a thing of beauty came out of such an ugly mother."

He touches her face, his own face still in the crook of her arm, and says, "I don't care that you're ugly." Yes, she is big and round, but he likes her largeness.

"You're just being a good son," she says, "saying nice things to your mother." She pulls him tighter into her. "You'll never abandon your mother, will you?" He shakes his head.

Since the curtains are drawn, the light in the room is muted. Evening is approaching. Noise from the outside filters in—traffic sounds, shouts of children playing on the street, snippets of conversation, a laugh or an exclamation.

Yet it feels as if he and Didi are in a cocoon that no one can penetrate. But soon it'll be time for others to return home. He doesn't know where she sends them to on these special Saturdays. It's as though she banishes them with the injunction to not even come near the house until the specified time. These days she locks the front door from the outside and comes in through a back door next to the kitchen, so that any visitor would think the whole family had gone out.

He wonders what goes through the minds of his father and Sumit. The Masterji knows what Didi does with Tarun, but there's nothing he can do about it. Tarun has no idea whether that smiling half brother of his suspects anything, for when he returns Sumit says, "*Dai*," with a pleasant face and talks to Tarun normally. The Masterji goes to his bed, pulls the blanket around him, shivering a bit even when it's not that cold. He doesn't meet Didi's or Tarun's eyes. He must smell their intimacy on the bed.

Amit asks Tarun for money when he visits. "Just a couple of rupees, *bhai*," he says. "You are the rich brother, I am the poor brother. What's the harm in funneling a rupee here and there? In your Lazimpat mansion it grows on trees, and we hear your Mahesh Uncle is planting even more trees." Tarun gets a weekly allowance of fifty rupees, so he doesn't mind sharing some with Amit. Sumit tells Tarun that Amit not only smokes ganja but also takes tablets called speed and Calmpose. In the last few months, Amit's aggression toward Tarun has stopped altogether. He's more ingratiating now, sometimes timing his appearance at Bangemudha on Saturdays to coincide with Tarun's visits. Then as soon as he gets some money from Tarun, he vanishes. Sometimes he winks at Tarun and tilts his head toward Didi.

After she visited her maternal home, Apsara stopped her walks into the city, as though that was the final straw. Tarun finds it hard to look at her. He's repulsed by her appearance. She looks like an emaciated street beggar. She's lost so much weight her cheeks have no flesh, only two bones jutting out like rocks. Her eye sockets have retreated into her skull, so her eyes look like they're floating in black space. She has lost control over her lower lip because it hangs down in a perpetual pout. She sits on a rocking chair, softly rocking back and forth, staring at a place in her mind. Sanmaya takes care of her, delivers her food, helps her with a change of clothes, makes sure she goes to the bathroom.

When Tarun returns home from his private time with Didi, his mother recoils from him, as though she knows what he's been up to. This makes him avoid her room for days. At times he even wishes that she were dead, then feels guilty that he does. When he thinks of Didi, he feels a gradual, warm arousal, and he closes his eyes and remembers her kisses, so succulent and loving, and he compares her lips with his mother's dry lips. Slowly he starts playing with his penis, and soon his palm is covered with his discharge. He has a tattered vest under his mattress he uses to wipe himself.

Mahesh Uncle doesn't understand why he is neglecting

his mother, and confusion shows on his face. He suspects that it's got to do with his complex relationship with Bange-mudha. Tarun is reticent and vague about what he does in Bangemudha when he visits on Saturdays. Didi adores him, this much Mahesh Uncle has gathered, but whenever Mahesh Uncle asks Tarun to invite his Bangemudha family to lunch in Lazimpat, Tarun demurs. One time Tarun said, "It's probably best if we let the two sides remain separate." When Mahesh Uncle said that he found it incredible that he's yet to meet the Masterji and Didi, Tarun said, "I don't know what good that will do. Why make things further complicated?"

So Mahesh Uncle stops asking Tarun about Bangemudha. He reaches the conclusion that it's too burdensome for a young teenager to be constantly thinking about his strange family dynamics and his mentally ill mother. The boy needs a life, too, doesn't he? But it worries Mahesh Uncle that Tarun has a tendency toward being a recluse. He does all right in school, brings home good reports, yet he spends long hours inside his room.

On some days Mahesh Uncle takes Tarun with him to the Mahesh Enterprises office in Putalisadak. He teaches the boy to duplicate documents on the mimeograph machine, write brief reports on the typewriter, and on occasion he also sends him out to run errands, like fetching a file from a nearby business concern or making purchases from the stationery shop up the hill. Sometimes Mahesh Uncle takes Tarun with him to the guesthouse in

Thamel and lets him check in guests. The boy does well. He doesn't smile much, but he has a serious professionalism about him that belies his age.

One Saturday a year later, after she's wiped him, Didi brings up the topic of the girls who might be after him. Lately she's been commenting more on what a handsome boy he's turned into and how girls must be eyeing him. Her tone suggests that these girls are up to no good. Today she says that the SLC exams are approaching and that he must study hard and not be distracted. She's observing his face as she says this. "You're such a smart boy. It'd be a pity if you let one of these seductresses distract you from your studies. You don't want to end up like Amit. Look at him. He failed the SLC with such low marks last year. He barely comes home. When he does, he glowers at me, wheedles some money off his father, and leaves. What a complete waste."

For a moment she's silent. In his underwear, he's lying in bed, staring at the ceiling. His time with Didi was especially pleasurable today; it has been a few weeks since they've been alone, and he's been obsessively thinking about her—her hands, her tongue, her breasts—even as he was trying to study for the exams.

"You won't let any of these princesses distract you, will you?"

"Didi, I told you—"

"You don't have to lie to me." Her tone is prickly and accusatory.

"But I'm not lying. I don't like any of them. They're so immature. Silly. They're always chattering and giggling."

"They're good for nothing."

"I have no interest in them." He nuzzles against her.

"I know there's someone you like."

"Who?"

"I know."

"Who?" He turns over, props himself up on his elbows. His heart is thumping. There's this girl at the bus stop. He hasn't told anyone about her. Whom would he tell? This girl is thin, with bob-cut hair. She's usually standing across the street with other girls, waiting for her bus. He stands a bit apart from the boys at his bus stop. He secretly watches her, averting his gaze if she happens to look his way. One time she caught him looking at her, and he half expected her to march angrily across the street. Luna, she's called by her friends. He has repeated the name to himself at night. It's a strange name, but it seems to fit her, her angular body, her short hair and sharp features. He wonders what it would be like to have her as a girlfriend, and he knows that it will never happen. She'll recognize immediately what a depraved, sick boy he is, and she'll want nothing to do with him. Still, he enjoys small fantasies about being with her, nothing big: holding hands, talking about school.

"You think I don't know?" Didi says. "You think I'm a fool? Is that the kind of love you have for your mother?"

"But, Didi, it's nothing. I've only thought about her a couple of times."

"Who is she?"

"Just some silly girl. She's not important."

"What's her name?"

"Luna."

"Ah, a city name. She must be the type who's out and about."

"But, Didi—"

"Well, now that you have her, what do you need me for?"

His world is beginning to spin. Her face has changed. Her eyes are narrower; her face is tighter. She's no longer looking at him. She's on her way to withholding her affection, and his stomach is contracting, a coiling of muscles that'll keep tightening and that won't relent until her face softens in forgiveness. She turns away from him and faces the wall. He should have never brought up the girl. He shouldn't have even thought about the girl. He's a fool. Now he has ended up hurting Didi. It's all that stupid girl's fault. She and her silly hair and her dumb name and her coquettish ways.

He's whimpering a bit by now, apologizing to her, stroking her arm, pleading with her to look at him, telling her that she's just someone at the bus stop, that he really doesn't have any feelings for her. But she doesn't turn. She's immobile, like a sleeping elephant. He weeps, calls out her name, tells her that he'll purge thoughts of all girls from his mind.

He stands on the bed and bangs his head against the wall. When she doesn't budge, he bangs harder, repeatedly. The sound resembles the *thud-thud-thud* of someone hammering a nail. His forehead is sticky with blood, but he's determined not to stop. He needs to show her his repentance. She needs to know that he'd rather hurt himself than see her unhappy with him. She still doesn't turn, and, gritting his teeth, he bangs even harder. His head feels like a pumpkin, ready to crack open and shatter into pieces.

The bed lurches, and she's beside him, holding his head in her arms. He pushes against her so he can hurl himself at the wall again, but she is too strong for him. Blood from his forehead has trickled down to his eyes, making his vision blurred; it's also running down to his neck. Sharp, seizing pain is pulsating in his head, then shuddering through his spine. She's whispering things to him, planting kisses on him.

She has him lie down on the bed, then hurriedly fetches a wet towel, with which she cleans him. He closes his eyes as she inspects his injury. His forehead is swollen, he can tell without her saying anything. She rubs a cream on his forehead, then gets some gauze and wraps it around his head. She's silent, and her mannerisms resemble a mother taking care of an errant child. She hands him an aspirin, which he swallows with water. She makes kindly noises, then goes to the kitchen and makes some *kheer*. When it's ready, she spoon-feeds it to him.

When the Masterji and Sumit return home, they ask what happened. Didi scolds them for pestering him with questions when he's clearly hurt. "He tripped, the poor boy, and he fell, okay? Now leave him alone." Sumit goes to the corner to study, and the Masterji sits on the bed, dazed. He notices the speckles of blood on the bed; then his gaze falls upon the wall, where there's a crimson patch, with a few strands of hair sticking to it.

"Tripped and fell" is the story he provides to Mahesh Uncle and Sanmaya. That evening he runs a high fever. His mother comes into his room—Sanmaya must've told her—and stands by the bed, watching him. "I'm fine," he tells her, "you can go back to your room." But she continues to stand. Then she crumples to the floor, as though her legs have given out on her. He bolts from the bed and goes to her. She's shaking, her teeth rattling. But there are no tears in her eyes. She gazes into his face, and it's he who finds that his cheeks have become moist, and it's he who is consoling her, telling her everything is fine, that everything is going to be fine. He holds her tightly in his arms, and her fingers reach out, explore his face, attempt to wipe away his tears, but her fingers are trembling.

PART 2

CHAPTER TWELVE

NOW TWENTY-THREE YEARS old, Tarun has gotten into the habit of following women around the city. This usually happens after work, on the average of once every other week. He leaves the office of Mahesh Enterprises in Putalisadak and, telling the driver to take the car back home, walks. At some point he ends up following a woman. It's never planned; he doesn't have roaming eyes that settle on a target. He's not a hunter; he's not searching for prey. In fact, he suffers from the impression that he's the one preyed upon, by an unknown force that's constantly on his back. He doesn't need to turn his head to look—it's not that type of threat. It's more a brooding presence that hovers above his head. It's some type of a dance: he's following these women, and this thing is following him.

He doesn't even have to think about a woman during these walks. He's often thinking about something else. Mahesh Enterprises, for example. He's thinking about how to make the business grow again, for it has been declining in the last couple of years, ever since a senior manager absconded with a large sum of money, leaving Mahesh Uncle devastated and the company in doldrums.

When his mind is on Mahesh Enterprises and its troubles, there's a pensive quality to Tarun's evening walks. He's mulling the problems at work as he's meandering through streets and lanes. At a young age he's now the director of the company. The senior manager's betrayal has delivered a blow to Mahesh Uncle, and lately he has withdrawn from the company's activities and left Tarun to handle its day-to-day affairs. The plan for the five-star resort has failed because investors pulled out in the aftermath of Mahesh Enterprise's financial woes. The volume of import-export the company engages in has been reduced to half; so has the number of employees. Now Tarun oversees a staff of five at the Putalisadak office. He blames Mahesh Uncle's overgenerous personality: the old man trusted the senior manager, allowed him total access. Tarun has cut down on expenses that he thought were extravagant on Mahesh Uncle's part. He questions his staff when they take more than an hour's lunch break. He doesn't allow the new senior manager to handle large sums of money. He doesn't feel like he's an unreasonable boss: he compliments jobs well done; he's sympathetic, to a reasonable degree, toward his workers with family and children they need to attend to; and he allows his staff time off for major festivals, even if he has to take on extra work himself.

The older among the staff miss Mahesh Uncle, who makes only sporadic visits to Putalisadak. He knew the names of his workers' children. He held annual picnics to which family members were invited and where they were acknowledged by name. He gave his staff regular bonuses. He sent them on all-paid seminars and trainings. Tarun, on the other hand, doesn't get emotionally close to his workers. He's brisk, efficient; he can even laugh and convey a joke or two with his office staff. They go along, but they know he's different. There's a severely reserved quality to him, as though something is physically wrong inside; something about his body, the way it's so tight and contracted, as if, as one staff member put it, "there's a giant metal weight inside his chest that makes it impossible for him to feel joy." It's not that they dislike him, but they dislike it when they find themselves becoming sad in his presence, as they often do. He's a lonely figure: as he sits at his desk or when he's on the phone or when he studies a document or dictates a letter to the typist—even when he's drinking tea. The typist once complained to her husband at night, "When I have to spend more than a couple of hours taking dictations from him, I feel like my own world has become dark. Even the thought of him makes me depressed."

Tarun is aware that many people shy away from him. It's not hostility. It's a reaction akin to stepping back from someone with foul breath or with body odor. It makes him morose, his inability to connect with people, the "smell" he exudes. *You are a smelly, abhorrent person,* the voice inside him tells him, in a half-contemptuous, half-pitying tone. That is your lot. Yes, this is my lot, he acknowledges, and the thought brings a brief calm. He uses the line as a mantra: *This is my lot.* Sometimes it generates acceptance; sometimes an overwhelming sorrow.

Even during parties he finds himself either engaged in serious, short-lived conversations or by himself in a corner, nursing a drink. These days he's more or less stopped going to these parties, where businessmen drink heavily and brag about their accomplishments or complain about how hard it is to do business in this country. Now he only attends parties if not attending could jeopardize a business prospect. He is fine with working by himself in the office, his doors closed, handling transactions over the phone in which he can be clipped and concise and still get the job done. He's not sure he likes the world of business, the negotiations and the haggling and the *chaplusi* and the loudmouthed braggadocio. It's just not him. But he has taken on this responsibility from Mahesh Uncle, and he's going to fulfill it to the best of his ability.

"I hate to put you in this kind of position so early," Mahesh Uncle had said when he first proposed to make Tarun the director. "But I no longer have it in me to go to the office daily and handle the details. Every time I walk in, every time I look at the staff, I think of Biswa and his treachery, and I lose interest in everything."

"What's happened has happened. Biswa will get his due at some point. We need to move on."

Mahesh Uncle looked like he was about to weep. "I had such high hopes for Mahesh Enterprises, high hopes for what shape I'd leave it in for you."

"I'm fine with the shape it's in. I'll take care of it—I don't want you to worry."

His routine with Didi hasn't changed much over the years. When he goes to Bangemudha on Saturdays—now almost every Saturday—after some chitchat the Masterji and Sumit leave. Then it's him and Didi. He lies in bed. She exits, locks the door from the outside, then returns through the back door. He waits for her impatiently. She approaches him and undresses him, leaving him in his underwear. She often doesn't wear a bra so when she unbuttons her blouse he has full access to her breasts. The sickly pleasure of being with her is still the same for Tarun; if anything, it seems to have intensified because his libido has increased. She has learned to be even more patient, gentler, more teasing with her fingers so that his arousal is greater, and when he achieves orgasm he spurts more. She kisses better, her tongue performing more tricks, darting and taunting, sliding and attacking and submitting.

Over the years she hasn't aged. When he comments on

how she looks the same, how her skin has become even smoother, she says, touching his lips, "You've kept me young." He smiles, but he has been noticing more creams and lotions and oils inside cupboards and on tables, in the bathroom. Now during their love sessions she also puts on a lipstick-like substance that gives color to her lips and tastes like oranges or bubble gum when their lips meet. These days she likes to give him hickeys, which he covers with a scarf, even on hot days. One Saturday when the Masterji arrived home, by himself because Sumit had gone on an overnight trip with this college friends, Tarun forgot to cover the hickeys. His father, with concern, approached him and said, "Tarun, these red burns on your neck . . ." He trailed off once he realized what they were and, red faced, shuffled to the bathroom.

She also likes to call him her lover. "You've grown so much now," she says, "you're like my lover." She pronounces it *labar*. When she first said it, he'd laughed, for although he'd heard her utter Nepali versions of English words—*pilastic, taybul, restooran, iskool*—*labar* sounds too filmy. "Where did you hear it?" he asked her. She feigned offense. "Why? You don't think our types can use this word? Only your city seductresses can say it?"

He has considered going to see a therapist about what ails him. He has pictured himself lying on a couch while the therapist takes meticulous notes, saying, *Hmm, hmmm* or *Go on.* What would Tarun say to the therapist? *I was a young boy when we started our relationship. She is the only mother I've known.* This declaration alarms him. He has had his own mother all this time, so why would he say such a thing? Yet it's true: when he thinks, *Mother*, he thinks of Didi.

The therapist he ends up revealing everything to, in his fantasy, is a bearded man wearing glasses, with a grim visage. The man doesn't say much. He has a fair complexion: a foreign therapist. That's because it's easier for Tarun to confess to a stranger, someone from a faraway country.

He can't live without Didi—he knows this much. By the middle of the week, in anticipation of seeing her on Saturday, he starts getting headaches, and at night he thinks of her and masturbates in his room. Since his room is still sandwiched between his mother's and Mahesh Uncle's, he makes sure that no grunt escapes his throat. But by now, after years of practice with Didi, he has become good at holding in his breath. There's only a small *hmmmph* that emerges at the release, a sound like a clearing of his throat. He still uses frayed T-shirts for his discharge, hiding them under the mattress or in the locked cupboard; then, on an opportune day, he stuffs the T-shirt in his briefcase on the way to Mahesh Enterprises and flings it out to the small piles of garbage scattered throughout the city.

By Friday he's in a state of restlessness, so he goes to his mother's room and spends some time with her. She's usually propped up on her bed, a pillow behind her against the wall. He sits next to her and takes her hand. She's aware of his presence, but she doesn't react. Her gaze is locked on a picture on the wall of herself from her younger days, before she met the Masterji. There's a bubble of saliva on the corner of her lips, and Tarun takes the end of her dhoti and wipes it off. He talks with her for a while, softly, about what he did at work. It has occurred to him that he could reveal to her his big secret. Wouldn't that be something? As he clasps his mother's hand, he could tell her when it all started, what he and Didi do, providing for his mother small details that will be embroidered in her mind.

Of course, he'll never be so cruel to his mother, but there is the thought that she should know: after all, what are mothers for?

In the beginning during his college years, when he saw how his friends were chasing after one girl or another, he experienced some mild yearning. One day a girl in college passed a note to him in class, and when he looked up, she was smiling at him. Silly girl, he thought. Still, after class, hands in the pockets of his jeans, he went down to the spot where she'd asked him to come. Her smile was full of sugar when she asked him, "So, how do you like my note?"

He nodded.

"Did you think it was sweet?"

All the note had asked was to meet him down by the giant tree in the yard. "It was as sweet as *barfi*."

She laughed.

"So why did you call me here? What do you want to say to me?"

"Just to see what you'd do. Don't you like it that I called you here?"

The girl wanted him to go for tea with her. He doubted whether he wanted to go, but when she grabbed his hand and pulled him toward the street, he found it hard to say no. They sat in a tea shop near the campus. The girl talked animatedly, and he sipped his tea and listened. He liked her laughter but also thought that she was such a phony. He wondered how many guys she pulled into tea shops like this. In his mind he could easily picture her kissing and necking with one of the studs from college. Yes, she is like that, he thought. Then it occurred to him that Didi could see him with this girl. It was an absurd thought, for this was in Baghbazaar, the tea shop tucked in a corner with green curtains at the door. The likelihood of Didi passing by Baghbazaar at that hour, looking into the shop and catching him with the girl was ludicrously remote. But he could no longer concentrate on what the girl was saying—she became a face with moving lips. She kept saying, *"Hoina? . . . Hoina?"* and it was clear she didn't need an answer because she continued at full speed. He was facing the door, so as the girl talked his eyes kept traveling to the street. Once, he glimpsed the blurry figure of a big, round woman gliding past—it was more an *impression* of a person he saw in the gap between the curtains—and he crouched low and put his palms up to try to hide his face. The girl asked him what happened, and he lashed out at her, saying that he didn't have time for her drivel. He left her in the tea shop and went to the Mahesh

Enterprises office, which was just down the street, feeling ashamed at what had happened, that the girl had seen him cowering.

It has to be the right person. Often it's a young woman about his age, someone with a sensitive face, kind eyes, someone that he can talk to but knows he never will. It doesn't even have to be a college-aged woman. It can be someone slightly older, perhaps just a few years older than he, maybe a young housewife out running errands. There are days when it's not even necessary that he see the full face of the woman; simply a side profile will do, and he begins walking a few yards behind her. He maintains his distance—it's important that the women don't suspect any-thing, so he's as unobtrusive as possible. Thus far he's been able to conceal himself. Usually he holds them only in par-tial awareness of his eyes, as though they were somewhere around the edges of his consciousness. He's fully cognizant, during these walks, of the other pedestrians around him, the store signs, and the honking and blaring of the traffic on the street—they come into a sharp relief as the figure pulling him forward weaves in and out of the crowd, and he, too, does his own weaving. He's not stalking them: he never notes the house the woman has slipped into, never returns a day or two later to the area to see if he can spot her again. Once the woman reaches her destination, he leaves, returning the way he came or grabbing a taxi home.

It's in the privacy of his room that he then fantasizes

about the woman he's followed. He imagines that he and the woman have somehow gotten to know each other and have become attracted to each other. He imagines various ways in which this could happen. It could be a woman who has come to the Mahesh Enterprises office. They end up talking. He takes her out for samosas and tea, and that's how the relationship starts. Or he could be sitting in the lounge of the guesthouse in Thamel, tallying bills and consulting with the manager, when the woman would come in, escorting some foreign guests as their translator or guide. The woman would ask him a question, and that's how the conversation would begin. She'd end up sitting across from him in the lounge, and they'd talk late into the evening.

These fantasies continue for days. He and the woman are inseparable. They meet in restaurants, parks, at national monuments, museums, and temples. They kiss but only softly, never deep kissing or greedily sucking each other's tongues. They hold hands. They are tender with each other. And one day he pours out his shame. He tells her.

CHAPTER THIRTEEN

HE'S AFRAID THAT Didi will find out about his fantasies, so he keeps his mental meanderings tightly locked up inside him. Whom would he tell them to, anyway? He doesn't have friends with whom he feels comfortable sharing any secrets, let alone something like this. *What's wrong with you?* they'd say, these friends he doesn't have. *You're a good-looking guy, running a business at a young age. Women should be falling over themselves to be with you. You don't need to pursue these strange women in the streets. If you like someone, why don't you go talk to her?*

But he's content with his fantasies, the way he can shape them how he wants. He can decide where they're going to first meet, the first eye contact; he can dictate the pace at which the conversation takes place, the details of the museum or restaurant. He often finds that he has nothing to say to women that he actually meets, unless it's for business purposes, in which case he is professional and precise and nothing more.

He thinks of himself as a holder of secrets. The big secret is, of course, what's going on between him and Didi. Sometimes an image comes to him of her death, and he's drenched in heartrending grief.

He's ashamed of the improbable and ludicrous imaginings with his women, for what woman would listen to him admit that he sleeps with his stepmother, who masturbates him and lets him come in her hand? But these movies inside his mind console him, and alone in his bed he closes his eyes and just lets them happen. At times he wonders if Didi is going to catch him in the act, right when he's in the midst of one of these fantasies. It's strange—he isn't worried that he'll run into Didi when he's on the trail of one of these women. If he does, he'll have a ready and reasonable excuse for her: he's on an evening stroll or on his way to an appointment or out to buy a shirt. It's when he's alone, engrossed in his scenarios, that he fears Didi will catch him in the act. It puzzles him, for surely Didi can't read minds? And all of these are indeed happening inside his mind, aren't they? He never writes down any of his feelings—he's too frightened about what will come out or what others will discover if they find it—so there's no question of her chancing upon written descriptions of these fantasies. He never mentions other girls in front of Didi, not even the office girls who work in Mahesh Enterprises, for Didi is always very alert to the girls' names that might escape his mouth. In the past when he's merely mentioned a name or two, girls he barely even knows but who somehow feature in the conversation, a small tightness appears in Didi's smile. Then she might repeat the name of the girl again, something like "Priya Basnet. Hmmm. Where have I heard that name before. Have you mentioned that name before?" When he says no, she says, "I've heard someone mention her name before. It's not you? Are you sure you don't know her well?" She's not satisfied until he's vigorously denying more than peripheral knowledge of the girl.

"My life is ruined," Tarun says to Didi one afternoon.

"What is wrong with your life?"

"I'm a twenty-three-year-old boy sleeping with his mother."

These words have been lodged in his throat for some time now, but he had no idea that they'd shoot out of his mouth so impulsively, especially when he's with Didi. The hurt on her face is immediate, and guilt grabs him, claws into his chest.

"Do you think I seduced you?" she asks. "Do you think I'm a seductress? Like all these other girls? Like that so-called mother of yours?"

"No, Didi, you're not a seductress. That's not what I said."

"You think I seduced you into this?"

"I don't."

"Then you wish you were with one of these seductresses rather than me?"

"No, no, Didi, that's not what I mean. I'm just . . ." But the dread is building up inside him again, quickly, and it's moving up to his throat. He might have to harm himself again, like he did when he banged his head against the wall years ago, to prove his love for her. But, strangely, her face has softened, and crumpled. Is she crying? Yes, she is crying. How could he do this to her? How could he upset the only woman in his life who has loved him, the only one who probably ever will?

"You think what we're doing is wrong?" she asks, sobbing.

He's never seen her like this: she looks like a little girl who's just been made to cry by her brothers who called her fat and ugly. "Tarun, do you think, from your heart, that what we're doing is wrong?"

He's confused. What he said earlier had been building up inside him for weeks, and it had to do with a growing sense that he's been in a trap for so long that he can't see a way out. Yet now when she questions him like this, he's not sure that what he has with Didi is so wrong and suffocating after all. "No, I don't," he says.

"But that's what you're saying, aren't you?"

"I didn't mean it like that." He plants kisses on her forehead, her face.

She doesn't stop crying. "If you don't love me, who will be there to love me?"

"You know how much I love you."

"Then why are you wounding me with such words?"

"I promise I won't say them again. I never want to upset you, you know that."

Slowly her crying subsides. He wipes away her tears. She gazes at his face. "I don't care what the rest of the world says. I need you. You are my *labar*, and that's that."

"And you are my *labar*," he says.

Every other month Tarun gives Didi some cash, a couple thousand rupees, in an envelope. He usually hands it over in the kitchen, sliding up to her from behind and putting his arm over her shoulder with the envelope clasped between his fingers. With a smile, she says, "And what has my son brought me today?" even though she knows exactly what. "*Linusna,*" he urges, waving the envelope in front of her face. From his bed the Masterji has a partial view of the kitchen, so all he can see is Tarun clasping Didi from behind, his arm over her shoulder; the Masterji sees only a portion of her back.

"*Kina chhaiyo ra?*" Didi says. "It's not necessary."

"Here," he says, and gently pushes the envelope down her blouse.

She turns around to face him and says, "Why do you love your Didi so much?"

With a backward glance Tarun sees that his father is

intently observing a spot in front of him on the bed, his concentration so severe that it seems he's ready to shatter the world. The Masterji has lost a significant amount of weight: the skin on his face has rivulets, and there's no flesh on his arms. Most days he stays in bed, hacking and coughing. His chest ailments have never left him completely. The number of students he tutors has dwindled, with only an occasional young college-goer or two dropping by. To make up for the reduced income, Didi has found a job as a seamstress at Ladys Fashion in Pako, part-time work to bring some extra income to help with the rent. Money is tight.

Once in a while Amit shows up in Bangemudha when Tarun is there. He enters tottering or with glazed eyes. He, too, has lost much weight, so he's begun to resemble his father. In Amit, the Masterji has found the perfect person to vent his anger. His face becomes contorted, and he froths at the mouth when he sees Amit. "Take a look, take a look, what a worthless fellow. Are you happy? Are you a tourist in this house? And what nourishment have you imbibed today? Milk? Juice? Vitamins?" Most of the time Amit ignores him, but once in a while he says, "Shut your trap, old man." The Masterji then launches into another rant.

When Amit sees Tarun, he breaks into a large grin. "*Bhai*," he says and stumbles toward him and gives him a big, sentimental hug. "And how is my big-man brother? You're the only one, I swear, that I'm glad to see in this house anymore." He doesn't let go, and either Tarun has to pry him away from his body, or Didi has to say, "If you don't get off him soon he's going to start stinking like you." Amit loosens his grip and stares at Didi. Some days he smiles, as if to say, *What a wonderful creature she is.*

Amit draws Tarun aside, to a corner, and whispers, "*Bhai, alikati paisa bhaye dena ho. Sarai marka pareko chha.*"

Tarun knows what the money is for, but he doesn't demur, only asks how much Amit needs.

Amit acts surprised, "*Arré!* That I don't need to tell you. Whatever his highness can afford to give as baksheesh to his servant, the servant will accept."

"One rupee?"

"*Bhai*, why joke with me?"

Tarun dips into his pocket and withdraws a hundred rupees and gives them to him.

Amit takes the money and genuflects, then slips it into his pocket.

"Fleecing your brother?" Didi says.

"If it were up to him," the Masterji chimes in, "he'd rob each and every one of us blind."

Amit tilts his head toward the Masterji while winking at Tarun, as though to say: *You know what the old fart is about.* Then he tilts his head toward Didi and moves his eyebrows up and down at Tarun while grinning lewdly. "*La, la, masti chha, bhai,*" he says to Tarun, slapping him hard on the shoulder. "You have the life." His hand is still as tough as iron, and it hurts.

CHAPTER FOURTEEN

MAHESH UNCLE KNOWS that Saturday afternoons are reserved for Bangemudha, yet it's on a Saturday that he invites his guests. He informs Tarun only that morning. "Some people are coming over for a visit, Tarun," Mahesh Uncle says as Tarun is about to head to the office, from where he'll go to Bangemudha.

"Do you need to go to Putalisadak today?" Mahesh Uncle asks.

"Yes, I must take care of a couple of urgent matters. The bourbon shipment is also arriving this morning."

"Then come home around noon, okay?"

"Today is my day to go to Bangemudha."

"Well, come home, meet these people, and then go, okay?"

"Who are they?"

"Some friends of mine, not a big thing, but they really want to meet you." Observing Tarun's reluctance, he says, "Just for about an hour, then you can vanish."

"I was really hoping to go straight to Bangemudha from Putalisadak."

"Just one hour, okay, Tarun? I've already told them, and it'll be awkward if you're not here."

He doesn't understand who these people are, why Mahesh Uncle is insistent. But he says okay, thinking that he'll just call from the office later and say he can't come. But Mahesh Uncle phones him twice in Putalisadak to make sure that he's coming. After a quick trip to the airport, where he finds that he'll have to wait until next week to release his goods from customs, he returns home.

Mahesh Uncle is on the phone in his room upstairs, so Tarun waits in the living room. Sanmaya is in the kitchen, cooking furiously, and he wonders why Mahesh Uncle is being coy about the visitors. He goes up to tell Mahesh Uncle that he's already late for Bangemudha so he has to leave. Mahesh Uncle puts his palm over the phone receiver and says, "It's them on the phone. They're on their way and will be here any minute now. Please." Tarun goes to his room and lies down. He closes his eyes: by this time he'd already be in Bangemudha, and already Sumit and his father would have left the house, and he'd be alone with Didi. His body would be entangled with hers. He can taste her, and the ache in him for her is slowly rising. His hand moves down below his navel, but he can't arouse himself now, not with these guests of Mahesh Uncle coming. He has to save himself for later.

"Tarun! Tarun! Babu, *kahan harayo timi?*" He hears his mother call his name but her voice is blocked by a red mask with sharp white fangs. Whimpering, he opens his eyes. It's Sanmaya, her wrinkled face close to his, whispering, "The guests are here!"

He stares wide eyed at her in befuddlement.

"The guests. You are to go down immediately!"

He's still in his tie and shirt, but when he stands and looks at the mirror he discover that his hair is a mess. He opens his door and sneaks toward the bathroom. From the landing he hears Mahesh Uncle talking to the guests in the living room. Mahesh Uncle spots Tarun and signals him to hurry up. In the bathroom Tarun freshens up, combs his hair, then goes down.

As soon as he reaches the last step, he knows exactly what this is about. His impulse is to retreat upstairs or to quickly exit through the front door. But their eyes are already on him: Mahesh Uncle's, the father's, the mother's, and the girl's—yes, the girl. She's dressed in an orange sari; she has a serious face; she is pretty.

The father of the girl stands, then moves forward to shake Tarun's hand. The mother does a stiff *namaste*, and her eyes have taken in everything, from his crumpled shirt to the slouching posture. The smiling Sanmaya carefully carries a tray of tea and coffee and juice and biscuits and fritters.

She is wearing her best dhoti, one she wears only for special occasions. The elders engage in idle chat while the tea and biscuits are consumed. The girl sneaks glances at him. In Bangemudha, Didi must be watching the clock and wondering why he's not there. He can picture her dismay rising.

The conversation turns to Tarun. "I hear you're already handling most aspects of Mahesh Enterprises," the girl's father says between slurps of tea, the loudness of which elicits gentle elbow jabs from the mother.

"I'm doing what I can."

"And he's doing it remarkably well," Mahesh Uncle says. "I just wish we were doing better than we are, but, Shankarji, you know what the market is like. Still, I expect us to get roaring within a year or two under Tarun's able leadership." He smacks Tarun on the back.

It's a loud smack, and Tarun winces, which brings a smile to the girl's face.

"And you finished your intermediate recently?" Mahesh Uncle asks the girl.

She replies in a soft, sonorous voice, "Yes, now just waiting for the results."

"Tarun," Mahesh Uncle says. "Why don't you take Rukma out to the garden? You young people will have things in common to talk about. Whereas we fogies"—this elicits laughter—"will stay here and discuss our old-age concerns."

"Today was Bangemudha—"

"Go, go, it'll do both of you good to get some fresh air."

His reclusive tendencies have been a source of worry for Mahesh Uncle, Tarun knows this. "You should go out with your friends sometimes," Mahesh Uncle has said in the past. When Tarun spends long hours in the office, Mahesh Uncle says that the business doesn't need that much attention. "Just leave it be, Tarun. Some of these things will take care of themselves. Or let the managers handle them. I don't want you to lose all of your good years." Tarun doesn't tell him that he likes the solitude that work provides. He's unable to hold on to friends for long; they simply drift away.

"*Girlfriend-shirlfried chhaina?*" Mahesh Uncle had asked on several occasions, pretending he was joking.

"I don't have time."

"A young man like you—aren't you interested in girls?"

"I find them . . ." He didn't complete the sentence, for nothing that he could say would sound right. Besides, he himself doesn't know what he finds them. He finds them an enigma, a mystery, or he finds his own emotions about them a swirl of confusion. "*Alli kasto kasto lagchha,*" he said, which was a vague enough expression of discomfort that it would be interpreted in numerous ways. Then he said something that sounded right, that he might have read in a magazine, or heard in a movie. "Besides, the right woman has to come along."

Obviously Mahesh Uncle had been mulling that over, for soon thereafter he asked, "How will you know about the right woman without experimenting?"

"I'll know."

"What if I look for someone right on your behalf?"

Tarun hadn't answered.

Now this.

He and the girl step out to the Japanese garden. The day is somewhat cloudy, with the thunder rolling lazily in the distant hills. "What a nice garden," she says. Her face is slightly more open now, as though someone has let her out of her prison cell for fresh air. "You must spend quite some time here," she says to Tarun.

Tarun nods, says, "Yes, it's pleasant here." But one is expected to say more, so he says that he's so busy with work that he rarely comes out. He is aware of his mother's presence at the window, watching them. She must have been instructed to stay in her room by Mahesh Uncle, lest the girl's parents panic. It occurs to him that his mother might know more about this than he does. She might have been informed of who is coming, and given how she lurks behind the window she seems to realize that someone of consequence has been brought to the house.

"You seem lost in thoughts," the girl says.

"I have a slight headache."

"Not feeling well?"

"Just a small headache." He checks his watch unobtrusively, but she's noticed, because she says, "Do you have somewhere to go?"

He says no, and it's clear that she doesn't believe him. His chest tightens at the thought of what Didi is doing right now: she's sitting on the bed, facing the door, waiting for him.

They are standing next to a seating area with chairs and a table, but neither of them sits down. Her arms are crossed; she looks pensive, and she's avoiding his eyes. The silence stretches. Finally, the girl says that they should go back inside.

"Your wish," he says, "but we head back in now, those people in there will be scared witless."

His choice of words elicits a tiny smile. He asks her whether she likes the city.

"Yes, I like the city," she says. "Why shouldn't I? Don't you?"

To this he answers that he doesn't have a strong feeling either way.

"Then why ask me," she inquires, "when it doesn't seem to matter much to you?"

"I was just making conversation."

"Don't feel compelled to be chatty," she says with pursed lips. "We can stand here silently until you deem it appropriate to go back inside without scaring anyone. Witless."

He suspects Sanmaya is also peering out from the kitchen window that has a partial view of the garden. And in all likelihood Mahesh Uncle and this girl's parents are also stretching their necks to see how the two are faring. "Please sit," he says. "I'm not in a hurry to get anywhere."

She softens a bit at his tone. But her arms are still crossed at her chest. "It's not easy," she says, "this type of meeting."

"We might as well sit down for a few moments."

She does, slowly, as though she's unsure of what he'll say next and she might have to simply stand and leave.

"What aspirations do you have in life?" he asks clumsily. The words are very difficult for him because he has to pull them out from a dark pit inside his head. "I mean, what do you want to do once you complete your studies?"

She has sharp, intelligent eyes. There's also a type of sadness etched around them. Her controlled manner of sitting, the pulling together of her body, makes her seem as if she's posing for a portrait by a painter. Tarun has nothing to give her, and she'll soon be disappointed in him—of this he is certain. She's saying something to him, and he doesn't hear. "I'm sorry?" he says.

"You're not even listening to me," she says. "What's the point?"

"No, no, it's not that."

"I was saying that we live privileged lives. Well, at least you seem to live a privileged life, no? Is there anything you lack?" She waves her hand to mean the garden, the house. Then she's conciliatory. "I don't mean just you. I also meant to include me. We don't lack anything, yet there are thousands of people in this country who are leading painful lives because they lack something."

"You can't always measure—"

"Doesn't it amaze you that we happened to be born in one of the poorest countries on this earth"—he has a distinct impression that she's recited this combination of words often, to friends, at parties—"and here we are, can we truly, truly say that we have lacked anything for even a single day? Tell me honestly."

"Well, I—"

"I want to do something—something big that'll shatter this world, shatter me, shatter everyone around me, change me completely. But then I feel that I'm not up to it. It's just my little self going around in circles inside me, like a dog chasing its tail."

He loves the idea of being able to shatter the world. He thinks of this thin woman sitting next to him wielding a giant hammer, bursting open and releasing things that need to be let out. Something stirs in him, a glimmer. But he remembers how he's late for Bangemudha, how Didi must be beside herself by now, and whatever had tried to emerge retreats inside. This is mere conversation, with the colorful Japanese garden as a good backdrop for two people who are seemingly contemplating marriage. Soon this conversation will be over, and he'll head to Bangemudha. Yet what comes out of his mouth alarms him, making him regret it instantly, "So, have you ever been in love?" He's not sure why he asks her that; he's not interested in it—it's an inane question.

She's startled. "Have you?" There's caution in her voice.

He shakes his head. "What about you?"

"I can't tell you," she says. "It's too private."

She senses something and glances at the window, where she spots the shadowy figure. "Is that your mother?" she asks. "How is your mother? Is she doing all right?"

"She's as fine as she can be, I guess," he says. "It's no secret, what has happened to her." He wants to check what time it is but is afraid of offending the girl again, so he refrains. A knot is beginning to form in his stomach. He can see Didi, sitting at the edge of the bed, palms on knees.

Mahesh Uncle steps out. "*Kura sakyo?* Or do you two need more time?" he asks as he approaches.

In front of Mahesh Uncle the girl's body language changes, becomes more closed, tighter, more obedient.

"How do you like our garden, Rukma?"

"The garden is very nice, Uncle."

"And I think you look very nice in the garden."

They go into the living room, where there are more smiles. Rukma's parents and Mahesh Uncle seem to think that the encounter has gone well: the young couple has been observed to engage each other in the garden.

Sanmaya has emerged from the kitchen to bid goodbye to the visitors. Her toothless smile is more toothless, more joyous, today.

The upstairs door creaks open, then silence. Mahesh Uncle puts his arm around Rukma's shoulders and says, "Come," but her father is quick: "Is that *Apsaraji?* Since we are already here, it would be nice to meet her too. *Hoina hajur?*"

Mahesh Uncle looks a little uneasy. "Now, this is not a hidden matter." He lowers his voice. "You must have heard about her—"

"Of course we have. We all have problems, don't we,

Maheshji? I think a quick meeting with the mother will be good."

"Of course." Mahesh Uncle calls Tarun's mother, but there is no movement upstairs. Tarun is assigned to fetch her. He goes up: she is standing at the top of the landing and watching him. Her dhoti is crumpled, but her hair is combed. Did Sanmaya comb it in anticipation of the guests?

"Let's go down," he says. She doesn't put up any resistance. They descend the stairs. At the bottom she stops and stares, first at the father, who does a *namaste*, then at the mother, who smiles falsely, then the gaze settles on Rukma.

CHAPTER FIFTEEN

IT IS ALREADY dark when he reaches Bangemudha. Didi is in the kitchen, her back turned to him. Sumit is home. "Oho, *dai*," Sumit says with a pleased smile. He is so polite, Sumit, so happy. He has friends who care for him and want to spend time with him. His teachers at the college love him; the neighborhood shopkeepers give him a little extra—the butcher his choicest meat, the spice dealer a sample of a new fragrant spice. His smile doesn't leave him; he doesn't have a bitter, angry bone in his body. Even when the vagrant and drug-addled ways of his older brother come up in conversations Sumit says, "Yes, Amit *dai* is like that," as if to say, *What's the point of berating him?* If it's necessary to provide help to his troubled brother, Sumit does it quietly. One time Sumit brought Amit home late in the evening, Amit's face bruised and swollen. No one knows how Sumit got the news about his brother's condition, but he took care of his brother for two days, bringing him the hot-water bottle for his aching body, soothing him when he ranted, and applying iodine to his face, until Amit became better and vanished again.

"Why so late today, *dai*?" Sumit says. "Too much work?" He admires Tarun, has dropped by the office in Putalisadak a few times to watch him work. "How did *dai* learn all this?" he often says to Tarun. "You're so good when it comes to business matters."

Didi hasn't turned to him at the sound of his entry and his conversation with Sumit, so he goes to her. Sumit watches him go to her; if he thinks there's anything odd with the way Tarun and his mother interact, he doesn't show it. He may simply think that for some reason she has a bond with Tarun that's deeper than the one she has with her own sons. Sumit doesn't resent Tarun for it, and his affection toward his stepbrother hasn't diminished. There are days when Tarun thinks that such naïveté is foolish and dangerous. One day Sumit is going to be hit hard—either by what he discovers about his mother and his stepbrother or by something else—and it's going to destroy him.

In the kitchen, Didi doesn't speak to Tarun. He stands beside her, waiting. Until she turns to him and speaks with that special sweetness in her voice, he has to wait. There is no other choice. This is his life. He has chosen it, this union with Didi. It encloses him like a narrow steel cage, with so little room to move that his breath is forced back inside his gullet. "Didi," he whispers, and he remembers the blinding swiftness with which she dismissed his mother and sent her crawling and sniveling across town. He needs to touch her flesh, to press his lips against hers, to accept her lips, warm and nectarlike, on his face and cheeks and mouth and neck and bare shoulders. "Please. Will you please look at me?"

She doesn't, and he continues to writhe. It's his fault— this truth is so clear to him now that it's like a blinding white light. She hasn't yet eaten today because on Saturdays she waits to eat lunch with him. Every Saturday she feeds him first, watching him happily, then she eats as he fills her in on what has been happening throughout the week. But even as he is overwhelmed by his debilitating guilt, he fears that her withdrawal today isn't simply about his inexcusable lateness. It's as if she's sniffed out his choice of someone else over her. But how does she *know*?

Should he confess? Out of the corner of his eyes he notes that his father, sitting cross-legged on his bed, is staring at the wall, the one with the window facing the street, as though he's transfixed by a movie showing there. Sumit is sitting on a chair, engrossed in a book. He reads voraciously, that boy, and Tarun suspects that he writes poetry on the sly and has perhaps even published a poem or two under a pseudonym. Tarun briefly flirts with the notion of shutting the kitchen door so he can embrace Didi openly, make her face him, perhaps even plant a quick desperate kiss on her lips. But the kitchen door hasn't been pulled shut in years, and now it looks stubbornly stuck to the wall against which it rests. Besides, shutting this door would be a direct signal to the family about him and Didi. It will surely disturb Sumit, and, if he can help it, Tarun wants to spare his younger stepbrother any immediate suffering. The best thing to do now is to confess to Didi, let it all out so that she can then punish him, and it'll be over.

"What could I do, Didi?" he says. "I was getting ready to come here, when Mahesh Uncle brought these visitors."

There's no response from her.

"Please believe me, Didi, I really didn't want to meet her."

She stiffens, and the tiny hairs on her arms—is he imagining it?—rise. She still doesn't turn to him.

"He's worried about me," he says, referring to Mahesh Uncle. "I feel like I'm trapped."

"Who is she?"

Briefly he closes his eyes to savor the sound of her voice. She has given him an opening. But the battle is ahead of him now, and he knows it. He can't squander it away—he can't. "It's just some girl," he says dismissively.

"How do you know her?"

"I don't. Mahesh Uncle invited them, the family."

"Is that why you're late? Because you were *goofing* with her?"

"I wasn't goofing! I left at the first opportunity I could." He lifts his hand toward her arm, but she inches away from him so that his fingers get only a fleeting contact with her skin.

"So, what's the conclusion? You're not going to come here anymore? You're going to spend time with—with this . . ." Her distaste for this unknown woman is so great that she can't complete her sentence. "I can smell her on you. You let her touch you, didn't you? You let her do whatever she wanted with you." She leans her head back, as though he's reeking.

He's aware that Sumit has lifted his head from his reading, but the boy immediately returns to his book: this is the not the first time that Didi and Tarun have engaged in urgent whispers in the kitchen. "I didn't let her touch a single hair on my body. She means nothing to me."

"If she means nothing to you, then why did you leave me stranded here, alone in this . . ." She turns toward him, not to face him but only to indicate the flat, with her cuckolded husband and her smiling son.

"I will never let it happen again," he says. His feelings for her are so deep and true that they make him want to weep. All he wants to do is gaze at her, touch her lips with his fingers, inhale the faint powdery food smell that comes off her neck. It's crucial she understand how much she means to him and that he'll go to any length to . . . the picture appears before him without any effort: he and Didi in a room; the door is shut; there are no prying eyes.

It's clear, it's simple: now he knows what he needs to do.

"I have a surprise for you," he says. His voice is low, conspiratorial. "It's a gift."

"I don't need your gifts."

"Please let me do this. I want to see you happy."

Finally, finally, she turns to face him. Her eyes have a faint crimson streak in them as though she's been drinking. It's because of the hurt he's inflicted. "Next week," he says. "I'll take you to a special place." He knows exactly what he wants; he'll be able to secure it in a week.

She continues to stare at him. "And what about that woman?"

He moves closer to her and takes her hand. "She's nothing. She means nothing to me. I don't even remember her name."

The week that follows is a frenzy of two activities: finding a room in the city for him and Didi and resisting Mahesh Uncle, who is insistent that it's a mistake to let Rukma slip through their fingers. "Dart away from our palms" is the expression he uses. *Hatbata futkyobhane.* I'm not ready, he tells Mahesh Uncle, who is gently persuasive. "Once you get married, you won't regret it. Besides, who is asking you to give up anything?" Throughout the week he tells Tarun, "It'll cure your loneliness." Sanmaya, as she serves food in the dining room, chimes in: the girl's family is fabulous.

Tarun scours the city, looking for an appropriate place: a simple room for a few hours a week, if that, so nothing fancy, nothing that'll call attention to itself, an expense that

he'll not even need to record or justify. It'll be better if it's a
place close to where Didi works and lives so she won't have
to travel on a bus or in a taxi. He can't assign one of his
office staff to look for a place because he doesn't want any
questions or suspicions, so he canvasses the city himself. A
place close to where she works will allow her quick escapes.
On the fourth afternoon of his search, he finds a room at
the top of a building, which is so tall and thin that it seems
to be competing with Dharahara, the city tower which is
only a couple hundred meters away. The owner lives in the
next neighborhood.

The next day Tarun has a mattress and two chairs delivered to the room. They're rudimentary, the room and the
furnishings. The room is the only one on the top floor,
basically a single room on the flat roof. The owner informs
him that he ran out of money as he was constructing, so
more rooms will be added on this floor, but not for the
next couple years. The roof affords a nice view of the city:
the surrounding houses, the parade ground, and the thin,
white, pencil-like tower nearby. Tarun feels good about this
procurement; he is confident no one will discover them
here, in this room that's five or six stories up. It's in the
middle of the city's ruckus, with shops crammed into little spaces at the street level and street vendors hollering
and yodeling and poor migrant women walking around
begging with sickly looking babies in their arms. And the
mouth of the stairs that zigzag up the outside of the building is tucked away to the side. Who in their right mind

walking below would think that something is happening all the way at the top?

Didi will be pleased. Once the furniture is delivered, he walks around the roof. There are no railings to enclose the space, so, should he decide to leap, it's an easy drop. In a few seconds he could be a pile of blood and meat on the pavement below. It's late afternoon. There's not a shred of cloud in the sky. The noise of the city rises above with a small din, like a muted but energetic chant. He stands close to the edge and opens his arms wide and closes his eyes to feel the air.

At home, Sanmaya tells him as soon as he enters that his mother fell down the stairs and bruised her forehead. A doctor is looking at her upstairs, she tells him, and Mahesh Uncle is with her. Where were you? Sanmaya asks. We tried to reach you in Putalisadak, but you weren't there, and no one knew where you were.

He bounds up the stairs. His mother is lying on her bed, a bandage around her head. Her eyes are closed when he enters, but she opens them when she feels his presence. The doctor is sitting on a stool, writing. Mahesh Uncle tells Tarun there's nothing to worry about, just a minor concussion according to the doctor. Tarun sits on the bed, tired and guilty. He ought to have been here, or within reach. Thank god Mahesh Uncle was home. Tarun asks her how she's doing. He doesn't expect her to talk, as she hasn't talked for a long time, but today she says, "You get married now."

He looks at Mahesh Uncle in surprise and annoyance.

"I haven't told her anything, okay?" Mahesh Uncle says.

"You get better first, Ma," he says.

She clasps his hand and squeezes it. She's surprisingly strong, and it hurts.

"Why didn't you call Sanmaya up instead of going down the stairs yourself?" he scolds her. There's a buzzer next to her bed that she can use to summon Sanmaya from below. Apsara is staring at him intently. It's unsettling, her focus. Her nails dig into his hand as she whispers, "Rukma?"

Sanmaya must be filling her ears with the girl's name. Tarun can picture her, Sanmaya, standing next to his mother and talking, her knobbly, wrinkled, paper-thin fingers performing near her mother's ears, articulating for her those attributes of the girl that make her suited to this household. He panics at the thought of another meeting with Rukma.

"Bring Rukma here," Apsara says.

"Ma—"

Her right palm flies through the air and strikes him on the face. The disbelief of what has just happened stuns him.

Mahesh Uncle reprimands her, but she doesn't let go of Tarun's hand. "He's my son," she hisses to Mahesh Uncle.

During the night her condition worsens. She begins to breathe hoarsely. They gather in her room. There is talk of taking her to the hospital; there is talk of calling the doctor again. Tarun sits next to her and administers cold compresses to her forehead, even though fever is not an issue right now. As earlier, she is clasping his hand, but her grip is weak. Her eyes are slightly rolled up toward the ceiling. They continue to discuss taking her to the hospital, but there's also a reluctance, a sense that it might be better, in her case, to let nature take its course. She has suffered enough—this appears to be the silent understanding.

Just before she passes away at dawn, his mother looks at him steadily. "She's a good girl," she whispers. "A good girl."

CHAPTER SIXTEEN

THERE'S SOMETHING IRREVOCABLE about a dying person's last words. Tarun is determined to be firm, but as the days go by—as his mother's body is burned by the river, and he shaves his head and dons all-white clothes of mourning—her words ring in his ears, and her slap hovers around him, near his cheeks. Mahesh Uncle continues to pressure him. It's imperative, he says, to have a good female presence in the house. When Tarun can't argue with Mahesh Uncle's constant appeals any longer, he says, "Okay, okay, do what you need to do."

"Shall I make the arrangements, then?" Mahesh Uncle asks.

Tarun nods. He feels older, depleted.

The wedding is a quick, somber affair, in deference to the mother who has just passed away. Some people voice the concern that it's not allowed, and far from auspicious, for the son to get married so soon, within days of his mother's death. But the problem is, Mahesh Uncle points out, the mourning period lasts for a year, which is simply too long of a wait. It's Rukma's family that puts the pressure on. As sympathetic as we are to the loss, they say, we also have to think about our daughter. We cannot wait for a year. Who knows what'll happen in a year? Mahesh Uncle agrees. "After all," he says to Tarun, "it was your mother's wish that you get married to Rukma. I don't think your mother would mind if this process gets sped up." *I don't care*, is what Tarun thinks. He hasn't had a chance to go and visit Didi, and neither she nor his father has come by to offer their condolences—Mahesh Uncle had sent someone to notify them. He hadn't expected Didi to come, but he had hoped that the Masterji would show to pay his last respects to a woman he'd once so ardently loved. But he can picture the Masterji, sitting on that bed, wondering if he should go to the *aryaghat* where his second wife is being burned, checking Didi's face, wondering if she'd say, *If you need to go, go!* And in the end, just giving up and accepting the cup of tea that Didi hands to him.

Throughout the wedding ceremony, which takes place in the Dakshinkali Temple, Tarun wonders what he's going to say to Didi to justify what he's done. He doesn't want to think about how upset she'll be, how easily he's caved to Mahesh Uncle. This temple, on the outskirts of the city, was chosen because of its isolation. "Is there a need to invite people?" Mahesh Uncle had asked Tarun. "Should we have guests?" Mahesh Uncle answered his own question, saying that they should just go ahead and not bother with inviting anyone. Maybe they'll throw a party later. "But you might want to call the family from Bangemudha? No? I think the Masterji must be invited, even if he doesn't preside over the ceremony as your father. Otherwise he'll never forgive me."

Tarun said, "Let's simply not bother with anyone. Let's not make it complicated—get this thing over with."

Mahesh Uncle readily agreed, lest Tarun change his mind about the whole thing.

At Dakshinkali, Rukma arrives, already decked in her bridal sari, with her parents, and a couple of servants acting as attendants. She says hello to him. Hello! She doesn't act the demure bride; her face is open, yet her forehead is creased: like him, she appears perplexed by how fast they've moved ahead with the wedding. And—he's convinced of this—in all likelihood she doesn't want to get married to him. Yet here she is. Briefly, he imagines telling her, tonight, about his relationship with Didi. An all-out confession. That'll really hello her, won't it? He doesn't mean to be cruel to her. He realizes that he actually likes her, the small flashes of anger she shows, how honest her expressions are. But it's not going to work; that much he knows. He's already dreading tonight. He's already dreading her hand on him, her expectations, and it exasperates him that he's been put into this situation.

A young priest performs the ceremony. It's a hot day, with the sun on a gleeful rampage across the sky, and the shirt he has on seems to be made of some type of scratchy wool. Surrounding them are Rukma's parents and Mahesh Uncle and Sanmaya. The ceremony lasts only about two hours, with Mahesh Uncle urging the priest to move quickly, concentrate only on the essentials. "The crucial thing is that the groom and the bride are agreeable to this union," Rukma's father says. "The rest is just ritual." The relief and the happiness on her parents' faces are evident when the ceremony is over. They climb back up to the parking lot, where the parents hug Rukma and get into their cars. And Rukma gets into the car with Tarun. Now they are husband and wife. "That must have been the quickest wedding in the history of this country," she says as the car takes off.

That very night, he discovers the reason for the parents' concern: Rukma has recently come out of a messy affair— her lover ditched her—and the parents are afraid a leakage of that matter will stigmatize her for life. It is Rukma who tells him this, after they have gotten into bed. She clasps his hand and says she's tired. "Are you tired?" she asks. He nods, relieved. She puts her head on his chest. He doesn't know what to do, and immediately he thinks of Didi, what her reaction would be to this intimacy between him and his wife. His wife! He has a wife now. He can't even imagine what's going to happen tomorrow. He's so worried about how he'll explain himself to Didi that he's becoming numb. Meantime, it's clear that Rukma wants to talk.

CHAPTER SEVENTEEN

⁓

SHE HAS A past, Rukma tells Tarun that first night, and the past is not pretty. She had this lover, a Newar boy, for nearly a year, and her parents had no clue. Many of her friends had no idea that she was seeing someone. Two of her close friends knew, but she had sworn them to secrecy. Every day she was petrified that they would inadvertently let it slip, but they were good friends, and they managed to keep a tight lid.

There were days when she thought that all she needed to do was go to her parents, perhaps her mother, because she felt closer to her, and tell her that she had a Newar lover and that she loved him very much. Her parents were educated people; they were what she thought of as progressive.

They had Newar friends they socialized with. In fact, one of her father's closest friends was a Newar: the two went to school together, grew up together; he still visited the house. She thought that her parents would understand and that they would tell her that the world has changed and they are open-minded so they, too, have changed.

But one day Rukma's mother said something that made her doubt all that. They had been talking about the daughter of someone they knew who had eloped with her college classmate of a lower caste. The girl's parents were devastated. "She should have preserved herself," Rukma's mother said. Rukma thought that what she meant was that the girl should have stayed away from all boys, but later she began to wonder if in her mother's mind the girl should have preserved herself because the boy was of a low caste and that perhaps it wouldn't have been so bad if she'd vanished with a boy of the same caste. In Rukma's mother's mind, her own daughter would never stray from the straight and narrow. That's why they allowed her to socialize with boys and attend parties. Rukma is a good girl, her parents liked to say. And she was a good girl. She did very well in her studies, she didn't drink or smoke or dress provocatively, and she had, until her Newar lover, "preserved" herself.

Her Newar lover was a tall, wiry man with a mustache and the sweetest lips that she'd ever seen on a man. He was charming, a real seducer. That glistening mustache, those impeccable lips. He was soft-spoken, so much so that sometimes it was hard to hear him. In this city of loud and brash men, she loved that about him. He was a tourist guide, so he spoke a smattering of different languages, French, German, Spanish, and in the midst of talking to Rukma he'd move smoothly into another tongue, like, *Mon ami, mon chéri* or *Mi sei mancato molto.* They made her swoon, these exotic tongues, transported her to different landscapes, a European village in the mountains with narrow cobblestone pathways or giant castles perched on hilltops.

One day he ended up becoming engaged to someone his parents had chosen for him. That's when Rukma's mother found out about him. Rukma had composed a long letter to him about her devastation. She harbored hope that once he read her letter he'd see his error and return to her. After all, he was only engaged, not yet married. Her letter was nearly ten pages long. It detailed all the good times they'd had; it talked about the cruelty the society practiced by forcing people into castes and creeds.

Before Rukma could deliver the letter, her mother discovered it. Instead of getting angry, she wept in disappointment. Her father also moped around the house, didn't go to work, and spoke to her in delicate tones, as though his daughter were a fragile thing. Her mother handed the letter back to her, but how could Rukma send it now?

One day she saw her Newar lover in the market with his fiancée. He looked happier than he had been with Rukma. There was a shine to his face, an anticipation of the future, which was a clear signal that he wasn't coming back to her. He was showing his bride-to-be something hanging outside a shop—a dress, a hat, Rukma didn't remember—and the fiancée looked rapturous. He saw Rukma, right after he pointed at the merchandise. He spotted her across that narrow, busy lane. She must have been quite a sight for him. Her face was botched and swollen from bouts of crying; she had worn the same dress for days now, and her hair was tied in a knot at the top for some odd reason, possibly because she didn't want to bother combing it. She must have appeared like an apparition, the woman he had loved materializing out of thin air, with the shoppers' to-and-fro intermittently blocking the view. He might have thought that his mind was playing tricks on him. It gave him a small thrill, Rukma was sure, the sight of her watching him in a teeming marketplace—it made him aware of the kind of power he had. As he spoke to his fiancée he continued to look in Rukma's direction. A cow came and nudged his fiancée on the hip, a friendly poke that elicited gleeful alarm. "*Arré, arré, arré!*" said her Newar lover and pushed the cow away. His bride-to-be clung to him. A few bystanders laughed congenially, and he glanced in Rukma's direction as though ensuring that she witnessed his happiness.

Rukma tells Tarun that there are moments when she wonders if the mutual observation in the marketplace really happened. She was feverish and hallucinatory those days, and the marketplace incident could have been a waking dream, a result of her yearning-soaked memories of the past blurring with her fantasies of the future. It's quite possible that she saw someone like him, someone who resembled him, a twin-like Newar lover. After all, there are hundreds of mustached men with luscious lips in this town, aren't there? She might just have needed to see a replica of him in order to brush her hands clear of any remnants of that affair. As she went home, she might even have made promises and vows to herself: no more men, spinsterhood, focus on career, and so on. But once she reached home and faced the disappointed, miserable personas of her parents, she knew her resolve wasn't going to last.

"So, are you still seeing him?" at home her mother asked dolefully. "Is that where you're coming from?"

She shook her head. Her mother had been crying since the day she came upon the letter, and her eyes were red.

Rukma put her hand on her arm and said, "Mother, why are you crying so much. Let it go. It's over."

"That's what you say, but whenever you go out I think you've gone to see him—what can I do?"

She and her mother might have been in the kitchen then, and her father was within earshot, his hands in his pockets, his head down.

"He's marrying someone else."

"Yet the damage has been done."

"Rukma," her father said, "you realize, don't you, that once people hear about this, it will have very negative consequences. I don't even know where to begin . . ."

"What do you propose we do, father?" Rukma said. "I

can't undo what has happened. What do you think is the best solution to this?"

He was surprised, as though he didn't expect her to say it. Her mother stopped crying, and the two exchanged looks.

"Will you do what we ask you to do?"

Rukma knew what was coming. "Yes."

"Let us find you a boy, and let us move quickly before this gets out."

Her mother stood next to her, and now it was her hand on Rukma's arm, like they were playing a game of tag.

"That's fine with me."

"You're not joking?"

"I'm not joking."

She hugged Rukma. Her father uncharacteristically hugged her. More tears were shed. At that moment when she thought of her Newar lover it seemed like she'd known him a long, long time ago, whereas it hadn't been too long since their break up. How's that possible? Rukma asked Tarun. How can something that happened to her turn so fluid and flimsy within days? That's something she doesn't understand about this life. We become so wrapped up in, so intensely engaged with, our present moment, she says, and soon after the moment passes, its hold over us dissipates.

CHAPTER EIGHTEEN

THE SECOND NIGHT in bed when Rukma kisses him, he kisses back gingerly. He feels petrified, and his body is cold and unresponsive to her touch. After some light kissing, he gently pushes her away. It's not that he doesn't like the kiss; he's deathly afraid of what it'll turn into. "Is something wrong?" she asks, and he says that he's exhausted. She's satisfied with that answer, but when he gives the same answer on the third night, then the fourth and the fifth, a knot forms on her forehead. On the fifth night, she ignores what he says, and her hand roams his body as she attempts, unsuccessfully, a longer, deeper kiss with him, one with more feeling, the kind she clearly thinks a wife and a husband should be sharing. But he has an avoidance mechanism with the kiss, whereby after a few seconds he moves his lips and plants them on her forehead, as though he were kissing a sister. On the fifth night her hand rubs his crotch, and harder, with desperation, when she finds that there's no movement down there at all. All this time he's lying there stiff as a corpse, his heart pounding loudly like a gong inside him. *Please stop, please stop*, he thinks. *This is like rape*—this thought assaults him. *I am being raped*, and he jerks himself up from the bed and sits, facing the other way.

"What's wrong?" she asks him, her voice hoarse. She's trying not to cry.

He contemplates the floor.

"Did I do something wrong?"

"Nothing."

"Then why are you acting like this? Why—am I not— what is it that's my fault?"

"Who says it's your fault?"

"Then?"

"It's nothing."

"Is it because of my revelation? What I told you about my past?"

"It's not that."

After some silence she says, "I misjudged you. I thought by getting everything out in the open I'd gain your trust."

"It's not about your past."

She lies down and closes her eyes. He, too, lies down. He knew this was coming, and yet when it's here, it's worse than how he thought it'd be. The fifth night of their marriage and already there's an impasse so big it appears insurmountable. She is disappointed in him, and he simply wishes it'd all go away, that she wasn't here, that he had the bed to himself. He's not meant to be with anyone.

He closes his eyes, and here comes Didi, with her smile. She's giving him a bath, her strong hands rubbing soap on him. Her hand moves down to his crotch, gently fondling his penis. *No, no,* Tarun tells himself as he reaches down under the blanket and begins to stroke himself. This is the only way he can feel good right now, and there's nothing he can do to stop it. His hand moves faster. The bed creaks, but the pleasure is too intense for him to stop, and of course, as usual, he discharges quickly in his pajamas.

She's in disbelief over what has just happened, then she doubts herself, tries, desperately, to convince herself that she has imagined the squeaking of the bed. Surely, her new husband wouldn't be masturbating on the same bed after repeated failed attempts at sex with her?

He busies himself at work the next few days and finds some solace in the catching up he has to do. His mother's death and the wedding have pushed everything to the background. He has to make quick moves to salvage a couple of business deals and face one irate loan officer who claims he's in hot water with his bank because some key documents hadn't been signed on time. He makes phone calls and pacifies people and averts crises. His staff comes into his office, but he barely smiles as he accepts congratulations for his wedding. When a couple of them try jokes and innuendos about newlyweds with him, he's annoyed and responds with questions about their work.

Even as Tarun spends long hours at the office, the slobbering anxiety looms large in the background, his dread about Didi: what is he going to say to her about what he's done. During brief office breaks, he clasps his head with his hands. He thinks that he should have sneaked out during the mourning period or taken a brief moment before the wedding to explain what was happening, to ask for her forgiveness. Now the days are slipping by, and he's feeling as though small slithering things are crawling inside him, making him squirm. He yearns for her, shivers when he thinks of her face looking at him in adoration, her voice that's sweet as honey, her dark brown shoulders that he loves to plant his lips on. Didi lingers in the back of his head—people think of the recent dead watching over them, but here he is, having had barely any thought of his mother since her death.

In the house Rukma appears to converse normally with Mahesh Uncle and Sanmaya. During mealtimes she smiles and piles food onto Mahesh Uncle's plate, despite his protestations, like a good daughter-in-law should. In the kitchen she tucks the end of her dhoti into her waist and goes to work, cooking the favorite dishes of the men in the house, thereby receiving even-bigger toothless smiles of approval from Sanmaya.

But as days go by, it takes her longer to smile, a couple of seconds more to meet the eyes of the person addressing her. She's lost in thoughts more often, and when she and Tarun are together in the living room or the bedroom there are moments she seems to find solace in leaning back and simply closing her eyes.

A couple of Mahesh Uncle's friends throw parties on the newlyweds' behalf, and they attend these parties and act normal. Later at night in bed, when she asks him how he enjoyed the evening—they're still trying to converse, despite the strain—he says that these parties tire him, then turns his back to her and closes his eyes, hoping, praying, that she, under the influence of one or two glasses of wine she's consumed, won't attempt anything. He waits, and she doesn't lean over to rub his shoulder or chest. He's immensely relieved, yet despondent. He's sure that her thoughts are filled with her Newar lover.

A few weeks after his wedding he leaves Putalisadak early in the afternoon and goes to Ladys Fashion. The sewing shop is in a large room of the second floor of a house in Pako. He stands in the doorway, listening to the clacking and clattering of a dozen or so machines operated by women. Didi is in a corner, close to the window, and she doesn't look up from her work. The owner of the shop, a small woman with a large mole on her nose, greets him, and he nods and goes to Didi. In this moment of anxiety and trepidation as he approaches her, he finds it difficult to maintain his official face, a young man who is in charge of a company at twenty-three. What he really wants to do is crouch before her, in front of her machine, and ask for forgiveness. But eyes are watching them, so he pulls up a stool and sits next to her. "I wanted to come earlier," he says, "but I simply couldn't arrange it." Her eyes are glued to the thread that's hammering itself into the seam between her fingers. He keeps on with his low voice. She continues as though he's not there, and he, a married man now, briefly contemplates getting her attention by banging his head against the floor.

"Why did you come here?" she says finally, after an excruciatingly long time. Her voice is filled with days of crying. But she spoke, which means she's cracked a bit inside. He can even smell onions on her, faintly, from this morning's cooking. He savors that smell for a moment, then says, "I have something for you, something I need you to see."

"I don't have time to see your silly things." She bites off a thread with her teeth.

"It won't take long. Half an hour at the most."

She finally turns to face him. Her eyes are puffed up. Her cheeks slightly swollen. She turns back to her machine. He waits. The *clickety-clickety-clickety* of the sewing machines in the room—it sounds like there are thousands of them—fills his consciousness.

"You must be very happy with your—"

"I don't care about her."

She says nothing.

"I didn't come here to talk about her."

"Why?" She puts down the dress she's been sewing and faces him squarely. "Is it because you're having so much fun with her?" Her voice has risen slightly, attracting the attention of some women in the room. "Because she's so pretty?" It's as though she doesn't care if the others think it sounds like a lovers' quarrel.

He wants her to keep her voice down but doesn't want to jeopardize the fact that she's finally engaged him. He decides to use her language. "You know I don't care for these *sahariya* girls."

"Then why did you marry her, so soon after the death of your so-called mother, as if you couldn't wait to get your hands on her?"

"I had no choice."

"No choice," she says. Her voice is low now. "Did you think about me, for a moment? What my state will be?"

Tears have come to her eyes. He wipes them with his thumb, intensely aware that several pairs of eyes are on them. One of the women, a mousy one, has a small, knowing smile on her face.

"Please, *jauna ma sanga*," he says.

She's stopped running the machine. Apparently the whole thing had become too much for her.

"It's not far," he says. "I want to see you smile again. Please."

She presses her palm to her face. A man has entered the shop and is exchanging sharp words with the owner near the door, which has the other workers distracted. "Go wait for me downstairs," she says, with her palm still covering her face so that her voice is muffled.

Didi is quiet as he takes her to their hideout. Before they climb the stairs she says, "Where are we? Where are you taking me? If you're taking me to meet your new *chhaundi*, I'm not interested." But she knows his wife is not up there.

"It's a surprise."

On the second floor is a shop with copying and long-distance phoning facilities, and a young man there, his hands in his pockets, looks disinterestedly as they go up. It's hard to say what's on the next couple of floors—renters? shops?— but at one point she leans against him, breathing hard, and says, "Just a moment." By the time they reach the top she's so breathless that she's wheezing, and she keeps saying, "It better be good since you've made me suffer so much," but she finally has a trace of a smile, and her cheeks appear to have regained some color. He feels light and buoyant.

"Okay, what do you have here?" she asks, but the gleam in her eyes tells him that she's beginning to understand. He holds her hand and leads her past their room to the roof. His tie flutters in the wind. She surveys the scene. "Oh my, what a nice view," she says. "Is this what my betrayer son brought me to see?" But she knows there's more; she's simply playing along, like she used to when he was younger, when he used to lead her by the hand to some surprise, perhaps Sumit hiding behind the door.

With trembling fingers he opens the lock on the door,

and there it is, their sanctuary. It has a mattress and new sheets and pillows. There are two chairs, not expensive but decent looking and with padding. Next to the bed is a small table with a lamp; he doesn't expect them to be there after dark, but he doesn't want to rule it out entirely. His heart beats rapidly at the prospect of their staying here in each other's arms in the evening, as dusk falls over the city, with the knowledge that in Bangemudha his father will be waiting for Didi, and in Lazimpat Rukma will be wondering where he is.

"Tarun, what is this?" she says, standing at the door.

"For you," he says. His hand holding hers is damp, but he's unwilling to let it go. "*Bhitra aunusna.*"

"I'm afraid to," she says. Her voice is soft because she's so happy. "When did you do this?"

Tears roll down his cheeks. She quickly embraces him. "I didn't know my son had gone through so much trouble for me." She takes his face between her palms and implants fervent kisses, on his eyes, cheeks, neck, lips, where she lingers until he can no longer distinguish between his breath and hers. Their lips enjoined, she pulls him to the bed and lowers him, makes him lie down. Her lips still attached to his—the thought flashes through him that he'll never be able to extricate himself from her—she loosens his tie, unbuttons his shirt. Her right hand slips into his undershirt, and she plays with his nipples. Her lips finally let go of his—God, they feel mauled—and now they move down to his neck. She kisses and probes the soft parts of his neck, runs her tongue on his throat. She pushes up his *ganji* so she has access to his bare skin, and she lovingly licks and laps on his nipples. Her head moves down to his belly, his navel, where her tongue darts in and out, then burrows itself deep for a few seconds. He writhes and moans. Now her right hand is on his crotch, and she's lightly rubbing it. "Please, Didi," he says. Her tongue still flickering on his navel, she deftly unbuttons his trousers and pulls them down to his knees. In no time his underwear is down, too, and she's stroking his member. She brings her mouth up to his ear and whispers, "Does that wife of yours do this for you?"

He can't think—he doesn't care.

Her palm is sliding up and down his hardened penis. "Do you love her more than you love me, your mother?"

"No! No!" He's crying again.

"What will you tell her when you go home?"

"That I don't love her."

Her hand pauses.

"Please!"

"That won't be enough."

"Please, Didi, what should I tell her? Please don't stop."

"You know what to tell her."

"I'll tell her that I love you more than I love her."

Her fingers resume their play, and soon he arches his back and spurts his semen all over her palm, on the bed. "*La hera, la hera,*" she says as though he were a child who'd made a mess while eating. She reaches into her dowdy bag, pulls out a white handkerchief, and wipes him with great care.

Their bedroom turns into a painful space. At night Rukma changes into her nightgown in the bathroom, then slips into bed, still hoping that something will be different. He lingers in the living room, either reading or talking softly with Mahesh Uncle. Then the two men come up. Tarun enters their room, and she hears Mahesh Uncle shut his door. He, too, changes into his pajamas. He tries idle conversation with her, but she knows it's to mask the discomfort he feels. He slides into bed, and both of them lie quietly. She doesn't want to initiate anything because she feels that she's tried enough, that now it's his turn. And he doesn't want to start anything because he knows there will be no completion.

One night he takes her hand in his, strokes it. She won't look at his face because tears have come to her eyes, and she doesn't want to appear vulnerable to him. "I'm sorry," he whispers.

"I'm not right for you," she says.

"It's not that."

"You don't like me."

"No, no, you're wrong about that."

"It's not this, it's not that. Then what is it? Why are things the way they are?"

She takes his silence as proof that he considers her inadequate.

Every day he can see the small damaging effects he's having on her. He rationalizes then that she has also chosen her fate, which is to be with him, so she has no choice but to accept it. Just like he's had to accept his life with a step-mother with whom he's so tightly entangled. You are bound to your Newar lover and I am bound to Didi, that's our fate, he thinks. We can think of it as a marriage of convenience, a functional marriage.

Neither Mahesh Uncle nor Sanmaya nor her parents, who have visited a couple of times, have an inkling that anything is amiss. There are moments when he's assaulted by guilt regarding her, what she may be going through, and he thinks: Rukma, you should make it easy on your-self and leave me.

PART 3

CHAPTER NINETEEN

DAYS SLIDE BY, and she doesn't leave. She can't because she has no desire to make her parents suffer any more. What would she say to them? That something is not right with their marriage, with him? They would respond that it's too early, that her expectations are too high. Her mother, in her exasperation, may even comment that she should not expect it to be like her Newar lover, smooching lips and honey talk all day long. Her mother may even say, *Do you see the two of us, your father and mother, besotted with each other? Yet, no one can say that there's no love between us.* Her mother's example of the solidity and immovability of her own marital love is a self-enclosed argument: it doesn't tolerate exceptions and departures. In such a closed system, would it make a

difference to them when Rukma says that she and Tarun,
weeks past the wedding, barely embrace in the privacy of
their bedroom? Would it make a difference if they learn
that their daughter has yet to consummate her marriage?
Her parents may recognize that something is off, but they
will be loath to admit it. *It'll eventually work out,* they'll
say. *With some people it takes time.* Her mother, ignoring
her own discomfort, might even ask, *But surely there's some
amorous activity in bed? Some petting? Kissing?* She might
even blush at this bold conversation she's having with her
daughter.

And Rukma, too, can't imagine saying to her mother that
the kisses, if there are any, and there are hardly any anymore,
are perfunctory. *I am the one who has to crawl over to him
and put my hand on his body. He doesn't respond. I rub my
hand over his shoulder, his chest. If he turns toward me, there
is a vacant look in his eyes. I think of an animal who is playing
dead at the approach of a predator. I whisper his name. I lick
the skin around his neck and his earlobes, but either there is no
response or he moves farther away from me. I move my fingers
down to his belly, then farther down, but there is no movement,
not even a flicker. He lies there placidly like a mannequin. I
fondle him, first gently, then hard with annoyance. He lifts my
hand in the dim darkness and pushes it away, gently—he's a
gentleman about it!—then turns to the other side.*

She can't think of telling any of this to her mother. She
can't imagine telling her that when she's trying so desperately
with Tarun and he's not responding, she begins to think of

her Newar lover. Her Newar lover was, if anything, a master of licking and crooning and whispering sweet nothings. His fingers were soft and sensitive as they meandered over her body and touched and tormented her. He knew how to move forward boldly and to withdraw, to bring his breath close to her ear and tell her how special she was, and oh what would he do without her. He composed poems about her, and he read them to her with his lips burning with love.

Rukma can't imagine saying to her mother that one morning in bed she asked Tarun whether they should go see a doctor. She was careful to say "we" instead of "you."

"What for?" he asked, not meeting her gaze. He was fiddling with the radio.

"I don't know. Maybe there's something medical."

He found the station he was looking for. "You think it's a medical issue?" he asked.

"I don't know, Tarun," she said, raising her voice. "I just want to solve this."

He turned to her. "Look, I know you're having difficulties with me, but I don't want to visit any doctors."

She said nothing more.

There's a melancholy quality to his face. A sad child, that's what he looks like: shoulders hunched, eyes large and bewildered, trying to understand an incomprehensible and unpredictable world that has thrown him around quite a bit. She can't even imagine how disorienting and traumatic it must have been for him to move away from Bangemudha to Kupondole and to have his mother's mental state deteriorate so rapidly. But whenever she has prodded him about his childhood, he's been reticent.

One day when the two are in the living room she brings up the topic of his childhood. He tells her that in the end, things haven't turned out so badly for him, have they? Although Mahesh Enterprises suffered a blow, business has started to recover. He doesn't lack for money, and he has Mahesh Uncle as a father figure. When she asks him whether he misses his mother, he says that her mental illness prevented his mother from being present in his life when he needed her the most. His face becomes transformed. "Now Didi is my mother. She's everything."

The "everything" pinches her, but she decides to ignore it. "Aren't you going to take me to visit her?"

"One of these days."

"But, Tarun, it's been weeks since our wedding, and you yourself said that she's more like—"

"She's a bit possessive of me."

"Possessive?"

"Yes, she has a tendency toward—how shall I say it? She can be—"

"Jealous?"

"You could say that."

"Jealous of me? But I'm your wife."

"She just needs some time."

"What are you saying? I'm married to you, and she's like your mother. Wouldn't she also want to see me?"

He stands from the sofa and moves toward the stairs. "She's not ready for you."

She has to hide her hurt and shock because Mahesh Uncle has come down for tea. "What's the conversation between the newlyweds?" he asks. He still calls them newlyweds, even though close to seven weeks have passed since the wedding. "Nothing," she mumbles. Is Mahesh Uncle blind to the strained relationship she has with Tarun? But increasingly Mahesh Uncle does resemble a man who feels like his duties are done, both at work and at home. He lounges in his room all day, drinking his frothy coffee and listening to his *raag*. He has cut down on most of his social events. "I'm too old," he says, and he acts old, shuffling around the house in his robe, his back slightly stooped, holding a newspaper in his hand that he seems to read and reread throughout the day. When he comes down, he peers for long stretches at the Japanese garden. He's still attached to that garden but not enough for him to open the French windows and step out and muddy himself. When Tarun and Rukma sit with him in the living room, he is pleased but shortly afterward he goes upstairs, to give them privacy, Rukma presumes. This is your house, not mine, he appears to be conveying, and increasingly his demeanor is one of a long-term paying guest who is waiting for a message to come so he can pack his bags and leave. And Sanmaya—she is so giddy in her own world, so beside herself that her Tarun babu is married and that there's another woman in the house, that she is blind to clues about things not right between the couple. But Rukma can't blame her: her world has been one of men, of serving men and taking care of their needs. So it wouldn't cross her mind that the wife may be unhappy.

Out of the frying pan into the fire. From her Newar lover to this.

One morning she recalls the proclamations she made to Tarun during their first meeting, about the need to do something good in this world. Where had all that high philosophy gone? How quickly, wrapped up in her domestic drama, has she forgotten. There's nothing preventing her from getting up and going out. So that morning soon after Tarun goes to work, she leaves the house. Mahesh Uncle is still sleeping, and Sanmaya is singing and pottering around in the storage room when Rukma sneaks away.

She goes to a shelter near the temple of Pashupatinath. The shelter doesn't match the grandiose words she'd thrown at Tarun, but it matches the smallness inside her. She knows this place through a college friend, who brought her here about a year ago. The friend was an idealist, and Rukma was at that time swaying only to the love tunes of her Newar lover. She thought her friend, Sahara, was too giving, too self-punishing and austere, wanting no pleasure for herself. On the road to the main temple complex, it's a shelter to take care of the destitute, the sick, and the elderly. Either through a sense of cruelty or irony, one of the founders had named it Swarga. But it's far from the heaven its

name suggests. A dilapidated house that includes a large
veranda open to the gaze of passersby, it's filled with cries of
pain, mad ramblings, and open and festering wounds where
flies congregate. The air stinks. That day a year ago Sahara
immediately got to work: comforting an old woman whose
son had kicked her out of her home, encouraging a sick and
emaciated man to take his pills, inspecting a young girl who
was suspected of having been sexually abused by her uncle.
Rukma watched Sahara, then it became too much for her,
and she left. She phoned her Newar lover from a shop on
the way. As she went to meet him, an intense feeling of dislike arose in her toward the people she'd encountered at the
shelter, even as she understood that they were incapacitated
and needed help. This thought strode into her mind aggres-
sively: *I want no part of it. It's not my life! You bring what you
bring into this world, and you need to deal with it, by yourself.*

Now, visiting Swarga provides some solace. She goes there
in the afternoons, and just like Sahara did, she holds the
wrinkled hands of old people, talks to them in a calm voice
whether they comprehend her or not. One day she ends up
cleaning an old man who has been suffering from chronic
diarrhea. Usually there's another woman who performs
these low tasks, a taciturn woman who executes them with
an alarming serenity. But this woman isn't in today, and
here's this old man with soiled trousers. "*La, eta aunus,*"
Rukma commands him. He's squatting on the veranda,
and he stands with some difficulty and walks into the room

where there are a few other people in various forms of misery. Watery feces drip from his trousers; there's a big brown spot on his crotch area. She leads him to the inner room, which serves both as the kitchen and the bath, with one corner for a stove and pots and pans and the other with a tap. "*Suruwal kholnus*," she tells the old man when they reach the tap. With fumbling fingers he struggles with the string of his trousers. This goes on for a long time, so she reaches out and tries to pry open the knot. But she can't. So she kneels and uses her teeth to gnaw through one knot that's refusing to budge. The stench coming off his body makes her gag. The old man appears perplexed by her action, but he stands like a good patient, once in a while a soft *hmm* escaping his mouth. By the time she manages to get his trousers off his legs, her stomach is silently convulsing. She steps away from him and takes deep breaths.

She removes his soiled underwear and, using a couple of buckets, begins to wash him. His behind is splattered with his excrement, and diarrheal rivulets run down his legs. *I can't do this, I can't*, she tells herself—yet she continues to wash him. She rubs her index finger up and down his anus as she pours water over it. She soaps and rinses his scrotum. She washes his thighs and knees and ankles. *This is not my job, what is wrong with me, how pathetic my life has become*—these sentiments are at the forefront of her mind. But she continues bathing the old man until his skin shines. By the time the buckets are emptied twice, he is smiling. She wipes him off with a paper-thin towel that someone has briskly handed to her; she wraps it around his waist and asks him to stay put. She runs to the shop across the street, buys a pair of cheap trousers and a shirt (what better use does she have for the money?) and returns to Swarga. The old man breaks into a smile, and with his new clothes on him he puts his hand on top of her head in blessing. She laughs derisively. On her way back home she carries with her a small smile, one that gradually diminishes as she approaches Lazimpat.

Rukma goes to visit her parents. Her father has a couple of errands to run, so he leaves shortly. Her mother asks her how things are, but before Rukma can respond fully her mother starts complaining about her husband. Rukma offers counsel. After a while her mother stops her complaints and tells Rukma how happy she is for her daughter. "You are lucky. You have found a husband who doesn't give you any grief."

Didi asks Tarun to take her to a movie. He is surprised, for she has not expressed interest in movies before. She's aware of some of the popular actors, but she's snatched their names from conversations or from advertisement posters. "Come pick me up at work," she says. And when he goes to Ladys Fashion after work and observes her from the door, he is slightly taken aback by the amount of makeup she's applied to her face. She's also in a bright red sari, something she might have worn on her wedding day in the village. The owner comes to him and says, "You and Didi attending someone's wedding today? I've never seen her this decked up." He's slightly embarrassed and mumbles, "Something like that." Didi comes to Tarun, takes his hand in hers, and says to her boss, "Today my son and I, we have our own plans."

It's clear that she has thought of this outing as akin to a date. She sticks close to him when they stroll through the swarm of New Road toward Ranjana Cinema Hall. At one point, she even slips her hand into his. He likes it but is embarrassed by it, so he slowly pulls his hand away. Once they purchase the tickets inside the theater compound, she expresses a desire for *golgappa*. He takes her to the *golgappa* cart, where the vendor dips the wafer balls into a bucket of spiced water one at a time, and they eat them standing. Didi wants to be fed by Tarun, so she asks him to put the wafers into her mouth. She licks his finger as a girlfriend might. He looks around. He wonders what Rukma would think if she saw them now. Inside, in the dark theater in the back row against the wall, Didi kisses him deeply, as she kisses him in Bangemudha. He returns the kiss, and inter-mittently throughout the film they exchange kisses.

Rukma has lost touch with most of her college friends, a couple of whom have also married and are now engrossed in their own domestic lives. Two of her friends have gone abroad, to England and America, for further studies. With one or two remaining friends she occasionally talks on the phone, but their chirpy voices have begun to depress her, and the conversation fizzles out because she often doesn't have much to contribute. A friend makes plans for a reunion. But when she considers what that gathering might look like, she decides not to go. What will she talk about? The mountain-like silence between her and Tarun? When her friends delve into nostalgic remembrances of the past, will she walk out because she'll be reminded of how much she's lost? Besides, that younger Rukma, the one who spent hours shampooing and hennaing her hair, who liked eating *kulfi*, and going to upscale restaurants and dance parties, now appears to her as from the wrong end of a telescope, a figure so tiny it might as well be someone else. The Rukma that's most visible and present to her, in a twistedly painful way, is the Rukma with the Newar lover, and that Rukma, in her besottedness and her gaiety, is such a foolish Rukma, such a loser, that this Rukma has developed a strong revulsion toward her. So the gatherings that her friends organize occur without her.

Day by day the silence between Rukma and Tarun grows. They will be in the living room, for example, sitting on the same sofa, and he'll be busy reviewing some office documents or on the phone with someone, and she'll be reading a book or a magazine, or pretending to. She'll want to say something to him, but the words rise to her throat and linger, then descend to her chest, where they become lost in a confusing swirl. As the days go by, the silence deepens.

CHAPTER TWENTY

ON SWARGA'S VERANDA Rukma is trying to feed *jaulo* to a demented woman when she hears someone calling her name. She turns toward the streets; there is Sahara, the friend who initially brought her to Swarga. "I am so surprised to see you!" Sahara exclaims. She is wearing dark glasses, a pair of fancy trousers, and has a bright, glamorous shawl wrapped around her. In contrast, Rukma is in an old sari that, because it's seen so much use, has begun to resemble a dhoti now. How much difference a short time makes. When they came to Swarga last year Sahara was the one wearing the simplest of clothes, cheap jeans and a frayed shirt that Rukma had thought was a hand-me-down, whereas Rukma wore recently tailored pants with flared legs

and a tight waist and a kurta-like shirt that had been pur-
chased at a boutique in Durbar Marg.

"What are you doing here?" Rukma says to Sahara,
embarrassed to be caught like this, of the work that she's
doing, of her . . . poverty? What is she thinking? What ludicrous game is her mind playing against her?

"I had to pass by this area, and I needed a glimpse of
the Lord Pashupatinath before I get to my meeting. Then
I spotted you on the way back. How have you been? So?"
Sahara arches her eyebrows, indicating Swarga. The *jaulo* is
getting cold, but the woman Rukma is trying to feed it to
doesn't open her mouth.

Rukma takes a spoonful to the woman who pulls her
head back. Rukma wishes Sahara would simply move on,
but she doesn't, so she says, "It's good to see you, Sahara.
Where are you these days?"

Sahara steps up to the veranda, crouches down next to
Rukma, and takes off her glasses. She has blue eye shadow
on. "I work for an NGO that does literacy work. But forget
about me. What's with you? You hated it when I brought
you here, and now look at you."

"I enjoy it," Rukma says, but in such a grim manner that
she feels like laughing at herself.

It's Sahara who laughs. "What has happened? What's
wrong?"

Tears well up, so Rukma turns her face away. Sahara calls
for another person to come out and take over the feeding.
"Come, let's go somewhere where we can talk in privacy,"

she says to Rukma. Rukma asks her about her meeting, and Sahara says to the hell with it, she's tired of these NGO meetings anyway. "There is simply just a lot of talk, lot of blah-blah-blah, empower this and empower that, with money going into people's private pockets instead of the projects they are allotted for. I'm sick of it." She catches herself. "But I didn't come here to regale you with my NGO woes. I want to hear what has happened to you. I heard you got married to this young gun of a businessman. Why was I not invited? That's okay, I'm just joking—I heard later that you decided to wed the quiet way, which I approve of. People spend way too much money to get married, especially the parents of the brides, taking out huge loans to finance these lavish weddings. It's a disease, don't you think, Rukma? It makes me never want to get married. But who'd marry me, anyway? I'm too shrill for most of these men."

A man comes from inside to take over, and the two women go to a dank tea shop around the corner, where Sahara tries to pry from Rukma the reason for her unhappiness. But Rukma simply cannot allow herself to reveal her marital problems to a woman she barely knows, someone who was more of an acquaintance during college than a friend. So Rukma tells her nothing is wrong. Sahara gazes at Rukma's face intensely and asks whether it has anything to do with her Newar lover. "You were, if I remember correctly, smitten with this man. There were rumors—your confidants might not have been as discreet as you thought. What was his name?"

"It's not important," Rukma tell her.

Sahara thinks that Rukma's reluctance to bring his name to the surface is a strong sign that she still can't let go of him. "I knew it, I knew it," Sahara says excitedly, banging the table. "Ah, first love! Who can forget their first love?"

Rukma says nothing.

"Do you miss him?"

Rukma remains silent, which Sahara takes as a yes. Rukma doesn't know what she's getting out of misleading Sahara, who has been nothing but nice to her. The truth is, of course, that she's moved past her Newar lover. But she can't fault Sahara for thinking that her present unhappiness is a result of that unfulfilled love. Rukma, too, has scraped underneath her emotions to see if there are any remnants she's not aware of. She hasn't discovered any yearnings toward her Newar lover, but she has concluded this: despite what she'd thought earlier, there was something authentic about the swooning, swaying Rukma, ridiculously in love even when that love eventually was found to be not-love. Ultimately it turned out to have no substance, but while it was happening it was real, alive, and it made her happy and vibrant. She'd rather have that, even knowing it was illusory, than this dead black bird inside her now.

"Ah, Rukma," Sahara says, her palm flat against the table. "I don't know what to tell you." A pause. "I'm not married, and I don't intend to marry, so I can't offer you guidance. Have you spoken to your Newar lover since you separated?"

Rukma indicates no.

"I'm wondering," she says, "if there's also some helplessness in his situation, a *majboori* that forced him to marry someone of his own caste."

The idea intrigues Rukma, even though she's sure it's not true. But truth, with its allegiance to what's real and solid, is on the whole unappealing and dissatisfying. So it doesn't surprise her when what she says is this: "Do you suppose he's also thinking about me? Right now?"

Sahara's eyes become alert, and she quickly takes a measure of their surroundings, as though some NGO types might be listening in. "Hmmm," she says. "Let me consider this." But it's clear that she can barely contain herself over this idea of the Newar lover pining for Rukma. Her fingers are shaking above the table; there's something more happening here for her. "Hmm," she says. "It's possible, it's possible that he's also thinking about you." On the table a spoon glistens with a thin coat of grease. She picks it up and plays with it heedlessly. "How will you find out, though?"

"Find out what?"

"Whether he's thinking about you."

"How?"

"Well. I don't know."

"I can't possibly contact him."

"Hmm."

"I can't possibly go to his house."

Sahara stops fiddling with the spoon, which is a good thing because if she hadn't Rukma would have clamped her hand on top of hers to stop the fidget. Their gazes lock. "Rukma?" she says.

Rukma can feel it, a vigor that's slowly starting to hum through her body. "Yes, Sahara?"

With her eyes Sahara is following the trajectory of Rukma's thoughts, and she clasps Rukma's hands above the table and says, "Don't do anything foolish."

"What type of foolishness?"

"You know."

"I have no idea what you're talking about."

"You're not considering . . . ?"

"What am I considering? What?" Rukma stands. "I will do what I need to do."

Their tea is done, and as they exit the shop a cloud of flies follows them, buzzing around their faces as though arguing.

"Aren't you returning to Swarga?" Sahara asks.

Rukma shakes her head and marches up the hill toward the main thoroughfare. Sahara keeps pace with her, alternately trying to dissuade Rukma from her mission and giggling over what she imagines Rukma is going to do. It's clear to Rukma that Sahara hasn't had this much entertainment in a long time, and she just isn't willing to let go as Rukma moves toward the city's center, where her destination lies. On the way she tries to shake Sahara off, suggesting that she better attend the meeting where her NGO colleagues are waiting for her slide shows and charts and graphs that pinpoint the cause and proclaim the cure. But Sahara is so enamored of Rukma's little project now that reminders about her work obligations, duties to her country, are not registering. She's fallen into a trance, this Sahara, and now she's following closely at Rukma's heels, chattering into her ears. She's less like a modern, chic working woman and more like Sanmaya in Lazimpat, whose little world has its own customs and its own language. And as with Sanmaya, Rukma can't even make out what Sahara is saying. She is speaking gibberish, a mishmash of NGO language and entreaties and accolades with frequent forays into her own past with a brother who . . . committed suicide? Rukma can't be sure. As they enter the dense snarl of the inner city, Rukma stops paying attention to her, and she does indeed become like a servant, carrying on with her own low-key ramblings as she accompanies her mistress into the market.

At the mouth of the inner market Rukma pauses. She needs to orient herself. It has been a while since she's been to his neighborhood. He belongs to an old Newar family with a house built by a great-great-grandfather, a house that has been a mainstay of his family for generations. It's not a grand house—it's right on the street, with a crumbling façade, opposite an entrance to a Buddhist *bahal* that has been seized by pigeons who also fly to the roof of his house to poop. The house is at the edge of the street that then veers into the tourist district, and if you're not careful you can suddenly find yourself among high-priced curio shops and white-faced, wild-haired, scraggly foreigners with their impossible tongues. "It's this way," Rukma says, but she's saying it more for herself, not for her companion, who she wishes would simply drop away so she could be alone. But Sahara is not easily dissuaded, and now Rukma likens her, in her mind, to a beggar hounding her for baksheesh. Perhaps if Rukma gives her a coin she'll scoot away?

The swarm around them is like a mob. There are many angry people in the city. Rukma hadn't noticed the amount of rage that circulates here. People shove others out of the way as they stride toward their destinations. One man is holding a bunch of red radishes in his hand and shaking it at the vending *jyapu*, who is so enraged that he's not even looking at the face of his prospective customer. There's a fat man with his hands in the pockets of his trousers glaring at the passersby, looking for an excuse to pounce on somebody, anybody, and Rukma dares not meet his eyes. The housewife up in the window wearing a shawl is berating the young girl below. The young girl is justifying, rationalizing, pleading. Judging from the housewife's index finger peeking out of the shawl and moving softly in the air, the punishment for the girl will be severe and crippling.

This is the city Rukma lives in, and she becomes despondent just thinking of these people unwilling to relinquish their anger. But today she has a task to perform, and she can't dwell on distractions. She has to focus. Her every thought has to be sharp, like the ray of sun harnessed through a magnifying glass to burn insects.

Rukma spots the house and turns to Sahara. "You can't go in with me," Rukma says. Sahara pleads and begs, but Rukma is firm. "There's a tea shop in that alley." She points toward the *bahal.* "Go drink tea in there, watch the pigeons." And she actually ends up giving her, from her purse, a few rupees for tea. She knows of the shop because she'd spent time there with her Newar lover.

She waits until Sahara crosses the street, then pushes the door and enters. Inside, it is pitch dark. She's never set foot in the house. He never brought her here. Why would he? His family wouldn't have approved any more than hers. They knew he had a girl somewhere, but in their mind he was having a little bit of fun on the side with a doxy, and it'd all go away once they hooked him up with a nice girl from their own community. When Rukma had asked him once whether his parents would accept her, he'd said, "I'll make them." Their visits to the tea shop in the *bahal* lane across from his house were an adventure in a type of daring, or "getting you used to my neighborhood," as he liked to say.

CHAPTER TWENTY-ONE

"*KOI HUNUHUNCHHA?*" RUKMA asks in the darkness.

Someone responds from above, a woman, in Newari, and soon there's a rumble of footsteps down the stairs, and a flashlight shines on Rukma's face. She gives her Newar lover's name. The voice that comes from behind the flashlight is that of a young boy's, and gradually she can see the dim outline of his shape. He's a plump boy. There's a problem with the electric circuit down here, he says, that's why the ceiling light is not working. He takes Rukma upstairs, the first set of stairs, then the second, and at once she's in a large room. Her Newar lover is seated on the floor, his fingers about to lift food from a plate into his mouth. He's as handsome as she remembers. His bride—Rukma recognizes her immediately from the market—is about to ladle vegetables onto his plate. She appears to be a sweet woman, in all likelihood a virgin until she married, cloistered and sequestered by her parents and trained well in the culinary arts. Out of the corner of her eyes, through the window, Rukma sees Sahara across the street on a bench outside the tea shop, eyes fixed on the house. The window is small, but Rukma is sure her companion can see enough to fill in the blanks. It's like a small, personal theater for Sahara as she drinks her tea, watching Rukma rupture a domestic scene.

Upon Rukma's arrival, the Newar lover's hand holding a torn-off piece of *puri* and *tarkari* is in midair, with the gravy dripping *tap, tap, tap* below on the plate. His mouth is open in shock. The little boy, Rukma's usher, farts loudly, then disappears somewhere—the house is most likely cavernous and roomy inside even though it appears small and constricted from the outside. "It looks like I came at the right time," Rukma says. "Time for the afternoon *khaja*."

"*Timi?*" her Newar lover asks.

His bride asks him in Newari who Rukma is.

"I was just passing through. Do you recall the tea shop where we used to hang out?" Rukma points her finger toward the window, and across the street Sahara bolts up and places her hand on her chest, as if asking, *Me?* Rukma ignores her and turns her attention to him. Slack jawed, he fixes his gaze on Rukma, but it's less anger and discomfort than awe. He simply can't believe that Rukma is here, near the very bed where he makes love to his wife.

His wife's eyes are taking in every tiny gesture, each modulation of the voice of her husband and this stranger. She has turned red, as if she were the one about to be discovered with a compromised past.

"It surely is a surprise," the Newar lover says. "I hadn't expected that we two would meet in this manner."

"I saw the two of you in the market some time ago," Rukma says, pointing to the wife. "I had been wondering about you since then."

"Please sit," the wife says, unable to mask her displeasure but trying hard to be a good host. The wife indicates the cushion across from her husband, but Rukma says, "There's a bit of room here, so let me sit here, okay?" and she plops down on the cushion next to him. His wife says something in Newari to him; he tells her in Nepali to bring Rukma some food from the kitchen upstairs. The wife leaves.

"So?" Rukma says.

"What are you doing?" he whispers.

"What?" Rukma says. From her sitting position she can only see the telephone and the electric wires out of window. Sahara is down there by the tea shop, craning her neck, Rukma is sure, for a glimpse of something, anything.

"Are you out of your mind?" he says.

"What?" Her pretense at innocence pleases her. She wishes she had invited Sahara up and given her a camera so she could have snapped a picture of her during her *who, me?* act. Sahara could have also observed everything and reported each detail later. *Yes, I'd say that the way you sat*

down next to him could only be described as plopping down—
thyacchaa! And the wife's eyes did indeed get bugged out. Here,
I jotted down some notes: "Rukma's eyes wide like an innocent
damsel. Her Newar lover has a drop of gravy on his lovely mus-
tache."

"Should I not have come?" Rukma asks him. "Are you
angry with me? Should I go?"

He's still whispering, and frankly Rukma doesn't understand the need for secrecy. There's nothing hidden here.
"Why couldn't you have called me?" he whispers. "Don't
you see what a difficult . . . ?" His irritated whispers become
gentler. "Did you really want to see me?"

She tilts her head and transforms her face into a full-throt-
tled expression of endearment.

"Did you miss me?" he asks her.

He appears ready to kiss her, and it is in this pose—their
heads a few inches apart, his lips glistening—that his wife
finds them when she stands at the door with a plate of food
for Rukma. The wife strides in and bangs the plate down
in front of her. She says something to her husband in rap-
id-burst Newari. Rukma begins eating. The Newar lover is
eating slowly with an amused expression, conveying to his
wife that he is tolerating this charming but eccentric friend
from the past. Rukma tells the wife what good friends she
and the Newar lover were, then turns to him for confirmation, "*Friends*, no? We were very good *friends*, no?"

"Yes, we were good friends," the Newar lover mumbles
into his food.

"Your husband and I used to spend long hours together."

The wife has moved to the window, and, her face turned at an angle to them, she's looking out. Sahara must be beside herself at this clear view of the wife, whom she should have deduced by now has already suffered the initial blows. An idea comes to Rukma, and she stands, the fingers of her right hand sticky from the food, and she joins the wife at the window. Across the street Sahara is standing like a statue, eyes fixed on them. Sahara can see the strained face of the wife, Rukma's lips moving next to the wife's ears, although Sahara can't hear what Rukma is saying. Rukma is describing the hideaways in the city that her husband and Rukma used for their trysts: temples, parks, hillocks, paddies. She describes the brilliant flowers in the parks: lilies, daisies, roses, carnations, extra-large sunflowers. She details the motorcycle ride the Newar lover took her on, a circle around town, then to the ancient city where they hopped and skipped on the cobblestone pathways, and she slipped on the hay the farmers' wives had laid out to dry. "I thought I had broken a bone," Rukma tells the wife, "so your sweet husband picked me up and carried me back up to the central square with its soaring temple. People watched us and followed us because they didn't know why this handsome man was carrying this woman who was grimacing in pain; they thought a film was being shot." Rukma tells her about the time when the two of them had gone to the movies. In the dark theater a stranger sat next to Rukma, and as a melodramatic scene unfolded on the screen, the man sighed and put his arm on the back of Rukma's seat; his fingers rubbed her shoulder. Before she could complain, the Newar lover also put his arm across the back of her seat, and his hand found this stranger's hand. Then all hell broke loose.

Rukma licks her fingers, says that although she's enjoyed the company and the food, she's overstayed her welcome. The wife doesn't move from the window. She is already confusing loving moments she's spent with her husband with pictures Rukma has implanted in her mind: the whipping of the wind on the back of the motorcycle, the feel of his strong hips against her hips when he carries her up the hill toward the ancient city's square, the touch of his thigh against hers in seedy and secluded tea shops that dot the city. It'll get to the point where she won't be able to distinguish which experience is hers and which is Rukma's because he also has taken his wife to the ancient city and for rides on his Kawasaki 250 cc.

The Newar lover, still seated on the floor, looks defeated. He is realizing, perhaps, that he ought to have stopped Rukma. He's examining his wife anxiously. He accompanies Rukma down the stairs, holding the flashlight. At the bottom, he scolds her for revealing their past to his wife, then he attempts to embrace her, asks her when he can see her again. She tells him to come to her house so she can introduce him to her husband.

Rukma's journey home is, inexplicably, filled with sadness. She keeps recalling the wife, her peace destroyed. Sahara wants to accompany her all the way home, but Rukma is tired of her questions—"Were you telling her about me?" "What did his face look like when he first saw you?"—so after providing Sahara with some details she tells Sahara to go away. Sahara gives her a wounded look and says that she hopes Rukma won't forget to call her when she wants to do something like this again. Rukma knows Sahara won't be able to sleep tonight. She has also been changed by this experience, and the microcosmic moments of what occurred inside the Newar lover's house, the moment-by-moment unfolding—the flashlight suddenly shining on the ceiling to reveal spiderwebs; the rose-patterned sheet on the Newar lover's bed; the chubby boy's fart as he bounded away to play after showing Rukma in—all of these will seep into Sahara's brain through repeated playing until they begin to color the experiences that belong to her, that arise out of her own senses. She'll begin to think that she owns a rose-patterned bedsheet, or in the midst of an NGO meeting, the thought will appear that she has a chubby nephew to take to the doctor for his gastric problems.

By the time Rukma reaches Lazimpat, she is so filled with sadness that she can barely move. The guard asks her if everything is all right. She says it is. Tarun is in the living room, but she barely glances at him as she goes up. From the kitchen Sanmaya asks whether she needs a snack before dinner, which she says will be ready in an hour. Rukma doesn't have the energy to answer her. She goes to her room and lies down on the bed, but then she gets up and goes next door, to the room that her mother-in-law had occupied. Every few days Sanmaya dusts the room, so it's habitable. She lies down on the bed—it is smaller than the bed she shares with Tarun, but it feels comfortable. The room is also smaller, perfect for one person. She closes her eyes and soon drifts into sleep. She wakes up, briefly and groggily, to hear voices. They are talking about her, wondering where she went. "I saw her come in," Sanmaya says. "I peeked from the kitchen and saw her climb the stairs." Tarun concurs, says he saw her, too. Mahesh Uncle says—must be to Tarun—"I thought there was some sound in your room." It feels good to be talked about. She's like a child who's hiding in the perfect spot, smack in the middle of everything but concealed enough that no one can ever find her.

They look for her in the Japanese garden, they ask the guard if he's seen her leave the house, and finally with a worried air they eat dinner.

Later that night, Sanmaya discovers her in her mother-in-law's room.

CHAPTER TWENTY-TWO

It becomes her room. It's a natural transition. She likes how its size seems to match the cramped feeling inside her. She has stopped going to Swarga. When she contemplates taking care of all those people, this thought descends upon her: *Who is going to take care of me?*

She's also afraid of running into Sahara again. Soon after she visited the Newar lover's house, there were phone calls from Sahara, but Rukma refused to take them. Then Sahara came to Lazimpat, to the house. The guard sent Rukma a message upstairs that a woman was at the gate. "Tell her I'm not home," Rukma instructed Sanmaya, who inquired who it was. "An acquaintance who thinks she means more than she does," Rukma said. She went down to the living room, parted the curtains, and watched. Sahara was quarreling with the guard. Rukma couldn't make out the words, but Sahara's index finger kept pointing to the house.

"She's a fancy dresser," Sanmaya said.

"She feeds off other people's emotions," Rukma told her.

A few days later Sahara was at the gate again, and after nearly getting into fisticuffs with the guard, she broke down and cried out Rukma's name. "Shall I bring her inside?" Sanmaya asked. "Perhaps she'll go away if she just got a glimpse of your face."

Rukma shook her head. "You don't understand," she said. "That woman is insatiable. She's the epitome of greed."

The Newar lover also phoned, and she spoke to him. He sounded cocky and self-assured. He told her he had two tickets to a newly released movie. She told him she'd meet him at the theater, and she simply didn't go.

Mahesh Uncle is concerned about her. "It's not right," he says to her, "you sleeping in his mother's room. You and Tarun should sort out your differences." As he talks she notices how old he looks, with craggy lines running down his cheeks. He lives in his robe these days, an unlit, fat cigar between his fingers, as though it's an image he's copied from a gangster movie. He also neglects to comb his hair some days so when he stands in the doorway to her room—her mother-in-law's room that she's made her own now—he appears like someone who has wandered in from the street. But Mahesh Uncle is really not interested in the details of what's going on, is he? He might have a vague sense that it has something to do with Tarun's aloofness, but he's not sure why it has reached the point that they have to sleep in separate rooms. Rukma has heard him say to Tarun: Take her out, go and do things that young couples do. And yes, Tarun and she have gone on outings, have tried talking, but it's no use.

She's been contemplating, with increasing frequency, simply ending the marriage. She thinks these thoughts at night when the house is in deep sleep. She sits up in bed, without turning on the lights. She peers out at the darkness through the window. There's a hazy type of glimmer that's coming off the surface of the earth, and it makes the outlines of trees and bushes visible. She sees an apparition, a fluid figure, perhaps a female. A ghost. I've begun to see ghosts, she thinks bemusedly. Her mother-in-law, too, spent countless nights like this, staring into the dark, seeing her own brands of ghosts.

Today's ghost stands near the fountain, a woman ghost, her mother-in-law, Rukma is sure. Now, why are you there and not here? Rukma whispers. The figure turns toward the window, as though she has heard Rukma. All right, Rukma thinks, I've made you real. Let's see what you're going to do. Now the ghost is bending to smell flowers. Is that what ghosts do? Smell flowers at night? The ghost keeps looking in her direction after each smell, as though she's reminding Rukma of what she's missing. My dear *sasu*, my dear mother-in-law.

At some point she drifts into sleep. Tomorrow she'll tell her husband that she's moving away. Where, she doesn't know. She may return to her parents' house, if they'll take her. But they'll probably insist that her rightful station is with her husband. Has she tried everything to make her husband happy, to make her marriage work? Has she done enough self-analysis to see if she's contributing to the problem? She pictures her mother's weeping fits.

Instead of returning to her parents' home, she'll find a room in the city. She will return to work at Swarga. If the mood strikes her, she'll have an affair with her Newar lover.

Yet when dawn breaks, she is unable to move from her bed. Her muscles have become heavy, and the room closes in on her, and the walls oppress. She wants to shout for help, to call Sanmaya. But how much can Sanmaya do? She can't be at the beck and call of people all the time! It takes Rukma a long time to sit up in bed, like she's been drugged. In front of her is the old photograph of her mother-in-law from her younger days. It shows her in red high-heeled shoes and matching red lipstick. She is wearing bell-bottom pants that tighten at the crotch and flare absurdly at the bottom; she has on a tight shirt that makes her breasts protrude. The photo was taken about the time, or right before, she met the Masterji.

Holding the staircase railing, Rukma manages to go downstairs. Descending slowly, like an ill person, not unlike her mother-in-law during Rukma's first visit. She sees herself through her mother-in-law's eyes: innocent Rukma bruised by her Newar lover, half hopeful about a new life. There they are, the concerned parents, wanting to make everything right for their daughter, wanting so desperately to ensure that she doesn't suffer.

Rukma calls Sanmaya. She can hear her voice float away toward the kitchen, from where Sanmaya emerges. There's some exchange, but she's not sure what is being said. Now she's being led to the dining room table, where Sanmaya has her sit and says something like she'll be back in a jiffy. Out in the Japanese garden the sun is already so bright that the sky has turned white. It seems as though she herself has become older and slower and needs to be taken care of. And the person taking care of her returns from the kitchen, and a shaft of happiness enters her. Good old Sanmaya. What would she do without her? She asks Sanmaya something, but Sanmaya puts her tea on the table, spoons and stirs some sugar into it, and doesn't answer her. She must not have heard what Rukma asked, so Rukma asks again, but Sanmaya is busy now with her own monologue about the chores she has to do that day, a talk that's interspersed with how things were done in the village when she was a child and what the weather is going to be like and what festivals are coming up. Her voice is like the gentle patter of the rain, which makes Rukma think, briefly, that it's indeed raining, but when she looks outside there is no rain, only a blinding kind of whiteness.

The earlier resolve she had about leaving this house comes to her like a tiny bird with a message. Sanmaya brings her *pakoda* for breakfast, and suddenly Tarun and Mahesh Uncle are at the table also, demanding things of Sanmaya, rustling the newspaper, commenting on the weather. Mahesh Uncle—how come he's down here so early, and he's even dressed? He's flying to Biratnagar to see a dying aunt, he informs them. Tarun is eating quickly. He doesn't meet her gaze. He's in a rush to get to his office.

So what are you doing today, Rukma? Mahesh Uncle asks. Why don't you go to Tarun's office later, and you two can go out for lunch?

I am leaving this house for good today, Rukma says.

I won't have time for lunch today, Tarun says. Many things to take care of.

Why don't you take some time, Tarun, Mahesh Uncle says. It'll be good for the two of you to go out.

I'm looking for a flat today, Rukma says.

Not today, Mahesh Uncle, Tarun says. I simply can't do lunch today."

Or why don't you two come home for lunch, Sanmaya chimes in. I can cook something special. I'll even have the guard write up a menu, like in the hotels.

I'll be out all day looking for flats, Rukma says.

But it's clear no one has heard her, or no one is listening. Mahesh Uncle is asking her: Are you not feeling well? Why don't you go and lie down. Here, why don't you lie down on the sofa in the living room? Sanmaya will take care of you. Tarun, try to come home in the afternoon, okay? Rukma is not feeling well. I'll be back in two days.

At once the house is quiet, except for the sound of Sanmaya cleaning in the kitchen. Rukma is shivering. Her body is hot, burning, floating, yet it doesn't feel unpleasant. It's a different type of energy now, not quiet and closed but expanding, as if she's on her way to discovering something. The kitchen has gone silent. Perhaps Sanmaya is eating? Sanmaya is shy about her eating. No one sees when she eats or how. A few times when Rukma has entered the kitchen she's found Sanmaya in the corner, her back to the door. But Sanmaya immediately stops eating when she senses a presence. She doesn't even turn toward the intruder without first finishing chewing and swallowing. Come to think of it, Rukma has never seen her with food in her mouth. She has, however, seen Sanmaya drink water out of a *karuwa*. She raises the *karuwa* above her head, tilts up her chin, then allows the water to pour into her open mouth, the veins and muscles on her neck going up and down like pistons.

Rukma wishes that she'd been able to make Tarun and Mahesh Uncle hear her a while ago about her intention to leave. They should be given notice, put on alert, given time to recuperate, but they're not her landlords, nor she their tenant. She tried communicating it to them, and it didn't work. So, she'll first find a flat, then inform them. Tonight. She'll inform Tarun tonight, and he'll let Mahesh Uncle know when he returns.

It'll take too much effort to climb the stairs to her room

to change. She looks into the living room mirror. She's in the dhoti that she wore to bed last night, and with a pleasant shock she realizes that it's a dhoti that belongs to her mother-in-law. Now she remembers: when she'd moved into her mother-in-law's room she had noticed the deceased woman's clothes in the drawers. She was about to ask Sanmaya to give them to charity, but then she'd ended up picking up a dhoti—it might have been this one—and smelling it, wondering whether there'd be the scent of a dead person. But it had smelled good, faintly flowery, and it had felt soft in her hands, so she had pressed it against her cheek. She had remembered then that her mother-in-law had been wearing this dhoti when Rukma first visited. And last night somehow she had picked up this same dhoti to wear. It's little wonder, then, that now, gazing into the mirror, she thinks she resembles her mother-in-law. Even her hair is uncombed.

She walks out the front door. The guard observes her curiously but he opens the gate for her so she can venture into the blinding light of the city.

Where does one go in order to find rental flats? She moves toward the center of the city. She's aware of curious looks of passersby—her unkempt hair, her rumpled dhoti, her slippers—she came out in her slippers, and now she's going to pound the pavements in them!—all of these add up to an unsettled woman. She wonders what her parents would think of her if they were to encounter her now. Respectable people, they are—this picture doesn't fit the desperately managed image they have of themselves. She ought to rattle this perfect picture, just like she did with her Newar lover. She ought to visit her parents. But today she's not feeling like a rebel, merely someone seeking direction.

There's noise behind her. A festival. A large procession is rapidly gaining on her, and no matter how hard she tries she cannot move out of its way fast enough. The procession barrels down on her, a stampede of feet and arms, a clash of cymbals and pounding of drums, with shouting and yelling that are meant to be chants but resonate as cries of anger and vengeance rising up to the narrow patch of the sky and the rooftops that float above. She's picked up and hurled in the air, and she rapidly glides forward on top of a thrust of arms, hands, fingers, and thumbs, like a star football player who's being fêted for securing an impossible goal. The roar of the crowd reaches the onlookers cramped in the windows of these ancient houses. Because there are seven or eight people per window, some of them are hanging from the windowsills precariously, like monkeys. If they fall down, Rukma thinks, as she is ecstatically hopped above the caterpillar hands of the revelers, they, too, will ride the crowd like her. The people are so jam-packed that all Rukma sees are heads, a sea of heads. A chariot looms ahead, but she can't be sure it's a chariot. It could just be people climbing one another for a view or to construct a human pyramid. She imagines herself a queen, being honored and celebrated by her subjects. Then she is hurtled up in the air—a loud *aaahhhhh* erupts from the crowd—and she's jettisoned to a side lane, where she lands with a thud.

The lane is nearly deserted because everyone has gone to watch the procession. A couple of people walking by observe her with sympathy; they think she's a down-and-out woman cast aside by her family, like the old folk she ministered to at Swarga. As the festival moves away, the raucous sound in and around her ears also diminishes.

Two thoughts come to her in rapid succession. The first is that she could find a modest room in this part of the city, live with the common, dust-and-bones people who work with their hands and go wild with their celebrations. Maybe this is the life she ought to be living, among the average folk. She can find a job, then spend time at Swarga. She can return home tired after a day's work, listen to her radio, make friends, commiserate with her neighbors, dance during the festivities, watch the passersby from her windows, and call out to them. Immediately at the heel of this thought comes another thought, barreling down, knocking the first thought away: This is Bangemudha. Tarun's first family, including the infamous Didi, lives on this lane. God! Where has she landed? She meant to move away from him, and here she is deeper in his past.

She stands and dusts herself. A laborer carrying farm equipment stops and stares. "What are you looking at?" she barks at him, but he doesn't budge. "Don't you have work to do?" she asks, but moves on without waiting for an answer.

Now she *has* to. How can she not? She's right here, isn't

she? She recalls, almost with relish, that he told her Didi wasn't yet ready for her. Well, here Rukma is, isn't she? She has been literally thrown into this lane. Ready or not, here I come.

How to find the house? Ah, the Masterji. Everyone should know about the famous Masterji, even though his glory has greatly diminished now. But this is a city where legends remain in circulation long past their expiration date, so when she stops to ask at a shop about the Masterji, the bored shopkeeper tells her his house is at the end of the lane. "The one who married twice?" the shopkeeper asks to confirm, and she nods. "Yes, down this way. It's a one-story house with a small front yard." It's dusk now, with a haze in the air that makes it hard to distinguish what is smog and what is mist. Lights have begun flickering in the dwellings and shops around her. As she approaches the end of the lane, she sees the house. She slows down. The first room in view is the kitchen, which has a window, about ten or fifteen yards away from her, that allows her a glimpse of what's inside. A woman is working. She's a heavyset woman. There's a sizzle—she's frying—then the shrill blast of a pressure cooker.

The woman looks up. Their gazes lock. She has a round, fattish dark face; her eyes are big. The woman doesn't smile; neither does Rukma. The woman frowns; she's attempting to remember something; she's trying to figure out who Rukma is. Rukma strolls past the window as though she were only passing through. She can feel the eyes of the woman on her back even after she's moved away.

She's at the small gate of the house. She hesitates briefly, wondering whether she should go in, but she has nothing to lose. Let's see what's special about her. This visit might mean nothing, she realizes, for living apart from Tarun eventually could lead to divorce. The word sounds funny when she thinks of it, and she realizes that it'll be an anathema to many concerned. Even to Rukma it sounds like a big, grumbling, nasty, mythical beast. She hasn't thought that far ahead, only of separating, going her own way, living apart. If indeed this separation will soon culminate in a divorce, then what's the point of her going into this house?

Yet here she is, and inside is the legendary Didi whose hold on her husband is strong. Besides, the woman has already seen her, so Rukma is locked into going. She opens the gate, enters the yard, then walks up to the door and knocks.

CHAPTER TWENTY-THREE

A YOUNG MAN opens the door. He has a pleasant, smiling face. "*Kallai khojnu bha?*" A sweet voice.

"Is this Tarun's house?"

He laughs softly. "Tarun *dai* doesn't live here. Not anymore. Well, he hasn't lived here in ages." Then recognition dawns in this eyes. "*Bhauju ta hoina?*"

"Yes, I am Tarun's—"

The young man's happiness is palpable. "Oho, *bhauju, katabata?* Please, please, come in. How could I not recognize you, the fool that I am!"

"How did you recognize me, though?" she says, stepping in. "We've never met."

"I've seen your picture."

Her eyes take everything in: the sickly looking man sitting cross-legged on the bed. Then through the kitchen door, she glimpses the woman she's seen from the outside. Despite the voices at the door the woman hasn't turned around, and Rukma senses that she knows precisely who has come visiting.

"You must be Sumit," Rukma says. "I'm not disturbing you, am I?"

"No, no, of course not. You're not disturbing us at all," the young man says.

"*Ko?*" the man on the bed asks, lifting his finger.

She does a *namaste*; the old man returns it.

Sumit says, in a loud voice as though the old man is hard of hearing, "Our *bhauju*. Tarun *dai*'s bride."

A smile breaks on the old man's face, and he beckons her closer. The woman in the kitchen still hasn't turned; she has the excuse of the pressure cooker going off right at the moment when Sumit spoke, but Rukma is convinced she is simply biding her time. "Perhaps I've come at the wrong moment," Rukma says. "Isn't Didi at home? Tarun is always talking about her."

Sumit points to the woman, then goes to the kitchen and speaks to her. The woman responds in a low voice but doesn't turn.

"Come here, *buhari*," the Masterji says, and suddenly Rukma is sitting on the bed with him. "Let me feast my eyes on you." His happiness at seeing her is evident.

"I was passing through, then I thought that you all lived somewhere—"

Didi is standing in the kitchen doorway. "Oho, *buhari*," she says. She is smiling. "What brings you here?"

Rukma's words are disjointed. "I was . . . hadn't been able to come. After the wedding—"

"You mean Tarun didn't bring you here."

"I wanted to come."

"I know you did." She comes and stands before Rukma. The old man's smile lessens. Didi's eyes are large and penetrating. She sits down next to Rukma and takes her hand. "Let me look at you. Tarun *ko dulahi*. We finally get to see you." She lifts Rukma's chin with her finger. "I knew my Tarun would snag himself a beauty, the beautiful boy he himself is. And I hear you are from a very good family. We were not consulted on that matter, of course." There's a strong kitchen smell coming from Didi, yet strangely the smell and the stroke on the chin Rukma finds comforting, even lulling. "What are these circles under your eyes?" Didi asks. "A newly married woman like you, you should be hearty, healthy, and glowing, but why do you look like a withered flower? Is our Tarun not taking care of you?" Her words are measured, meaningful, as though she knows what Rukma is going through. "Are they not feeding you in that house? Well, no matter, today you've come here, and dinner is cooking, so you'll eat here." When Rukma demurs, Didi says, "I'll not accept no for an answer. You're already here, it's dark, and the dinner is about ready."

Sumit sits on the floor while Rukma continues to sit on the bed, flanked by the Masterji and Didi, with Didi's hands enveloping her hand. Sumit gazes up at her adoringly. He doesn't speak much, and when he does his voice is pleasing. "Your studies going well?" she asks him at one point, and he nods and says, "Going very well, *bhauju.*"

"So, tell us about yourself," Didi says.

Rukma fights the urge to spill it all out. But there's a coziness here that's illusory. "There's nothing to say."

"How's that possible?" Didi says. "An educated, beautiful city girl like you. Your parents must be very happy. Do you go to visit them often?"

"I go when I can."

"Tarun and I . . ." Didi doesn't finish her statement.

"Tarun visits you frequently, doesn't he?" Rukma asks.

Didi looks down at her hands.

"These days Tarun *dai* doesn't come as often as he used to," Sumit says.

"He's a busy boy," Didi says.

Rukma ends up eating with them, and eating ravenously. Every bite and every morsel—the mutton, the spinach, the *aloo ko achar,* the *titey karela*—is like an explosion of sensations on her tongue, and she hardly speaks as she devours the food. Since there's no dining table, they eat on the floor near the bed. The expert manner in which Sumit unfolds the newspapers and lays them on the rug, the quick efficiency with which Didi brings over the food, tells Rukma that this is where they eat their meals every day. Didi keeps ladling food on her steel plate, a large *khandethaal* that has separate pockets for each dish. "No, no," Rukma keeps saying yet continues to stuff herself. She's filled with a hunger that she's not experienced since her childhood, a greedy kind of hunger. By the time she's finished she is so full that she lets out an embarrassing burp. She can barely stand to rinse her hands and mouth at the tap, so Sumit helps her to her feet. "I should get going," she hears herself say, but there's a flurry of protests, Didi's, Sumit's, the old man's, and her own counterprotests.

"But you just ate—you can't leave now."

"Stay for a while, *bhauju.*"

"It's getting dark."

"You didn't bring your car?"

"No matter, Tarun can pick you up."

"I don't want to bother Tarun. I'll find a taxi, but if I don't leave now, there'll be no taxis."

"We know a taxi driver who lives in this neighborhood, not to worry. Stay a few minutes longer."

She's drowsy, and the next thing she knows she's lying on the Masterji's bed, and Didi is massaging her forehead. Rukma closes her eyes. Then her head is on Didi's lap, and it's all so very comfortable. The voices around her are muted, coming from a place beyond these walls or perhaps even from within her own mind.

"She's beautiful," Didi is saying.

"Tarun must be worried about her by now," the Masterji says.

"She's too beautiful," Didi says. "Too much."

Rukma's eyes open in the darkness, and in a moment of panic she thinks she's in Lazimpat, in her mother-in-law's room, until she feels a warm body against hers. By the heaviness of the breathing she can tell it's Didi. It's so dark that if she puts her hand out in front her, she won't be able to see it. She remembers: this was the bed where the Masterji was sleeping, and she's horrified that he's also sleeping here, with her and Didi. And where is Sumit? She stops breathing: he's not also on this bed, is he? Then she relaxes as she remembers that in the conversation before dinner it was mentioned that Sumit sleeps in the corner. Still, she needs to make sure, so she gingerly feels with her hand in the dark. They fall on a nose, a thick nose. She's reassured, yes, it's Didi, then she's worried again. She barely knows these people, and here she is, sleeping among them.

"He loves you very much, doesn't he?"

Didi's question startles her. Had she been awake all this time? "Did I wake you?" Rukma asks.

"I don't need to sleep much at night," Didi says. "You didn't answer me. He loves you very much, doesn't he, my Tarun?"

Rukma says nothing.

"You're a lucky woman."

"You might be luckier. He speaks highly of you."

After some silence Didi says, "He's always been special, that boy. He was so beautiful when he was little. You know, Rukma, I've always felt that he's come out of my own womb. Never felt that he was that Apsara Thapa's son. And now he's turned into such a handsome young man."

Rukma is silent.

"You should always keep that in mind," Didi says, "about what a special gift he is to you."

"Yes."

"You're not going to betray him, are you?"

"Betray?"

Didi's hands seek hers in the dark, and they clasp her fingers tightly. "Try to get some sleep," Didi says. "It's still dark out." But her fingers on Rukma's haven't relaxed, and it's becoming slightly painful now. "Sleep," Didi whispers, and Rukma closes her eyes despite the pain.

She wakes later to a grayish light seeping into the room. Her fingers are still entangled with Didi's, but the grip has loosened because Didi, judging from her breathing, has fallen asleep. Rukma quietly sits up, then grimacing at the creak of the bed, steps onto the floor. She can make out the shape of the old Masterji nearby, and she is startled to see that his eyes are open and looking at her. But he doesn't say anything. She tiptoes toward the door, where she stretches her eyes wide open to locate her shoes. When she unlatches the door and steps out, she's quite sure that Didi, too, has awoken and is studying her.

"We were so worried about you." Sanmaya is in tears. Her voice is shaking as she comes to the gate to meet Rukma.

"We thought that something terrible had happened. Tarun babu drove around at midnight looking for you. He called your parents, but he didn't want to alarm them, so he pretended that nothing was wrong. We nearly called the police."

Without answering Sanmaya, Rukma goes inside. Tarun is in the living room, the newspaper spread out before him. "I didn't sleep all night," he says.

She stands at the bottom of the stairs, her palm covering the knob at the end of the balustrade. Sanmaya has remained outside to allow the two of them a private moment. But tiredness has come over Rukma, so she makes a move to go upstairs, to crawl into her bed.

"You should call your parents," he says. "They're anxious."

"Later," she says. It's clear that he's trying to downplay his own anxiety and confusion over her absence, but it's too late. He stands, and he wants to say something. She's sure he suspects she spent the night with her Newar lover.

Later that morning she wakes up to voices downstairs. Sanmaya knocks on her door. "Your parents are here," she says. Rukma opens the door, her brain cloudy from sleep.

"I'll be down," she informs Sanmaya. She freshens up in the bathroom, quickly changes into a fresh dhoti, and goes down. Her parents rise from the sofa when they see her. "Where were you last night, Rukma? We were worried sick." Tarun, sitting next to them, cannot meet her gaze.

"I ended up staying the night at a friend's house. It was

too late to come home." No one believes her, but she doesn't feel obligated to be convincing to any of them. She instructs Sanmaya to make tea. Her parents say that it's nearly lunch-time, so they won't stay for tea. Rukma doesn't listen and goes to the kitchen to see what snacks she can offer them. Her mother follows her, asks her with a whisper what has happened. "I told you, at a friend's place," Rukma says, meeting her mother's eyes squarely. "What other answer do you want?" Her mother takes her by the arm and pulls her out to the Japanese garden, which seems to be the backdrop of everything significant that happens in this house.

"Did you two have a fight?" her mother is asking.

"No, no fight."

"Did he say something? Did he do something?"

"There's nothing wrong, Mother. Let's go inside and drink some tea. Father must be waiting."

"What is a married woman doing spending the night elsewhere?" her mother says angrily. "What will people think?"

"Mother," she says wearily.

"Is there someone? That Newar boy?"

Sanmaya saves her. She comes out to the garden, informs them that the tea is getting cold. "They're waiting inside," Sanmaya adds.

Inside, her father advises her to take care of her health. "Your eyes," he says. "They're swollen."

After her parents leave, Tarun asks her to sit down next to him. She does, but there's nothing to talk about. He's going over some thoughts in his mind, the precise nature of which she'll never know. When he looks at her, she catches a fleeting expression of desperation on his face, as though he's asking her to understand. "Inform me," he says in a halting voice, "when you're going to spend the night at a friend's place. That way no one here will worry." She takes it that he's accepted she's going out to spend time with someone else, perhaps her Newar lover. It's as though he recognizes that he's failed to give her the minimum that a wife would need. He looks defeated, so crestfallen that she stifles the urge to put her hand on his chin and say that perhaps they can work on this more. But they're past that stage now. It's too late.

CHAPTER TWENTY-FOUR

I T H A S H E R sitting upright in bed that night, this
thought that makes her wonder why it didn't occur to her
before: he has a mistress. Yet when this thought comes, it
seizes her with its logical force. It explains his disinterest in
her, the guilt that appears to assail him at moments. There's
someone else who satisfies him, both emotionally and sexually. It's quite possible that he's even married to her already.
Rukma laughs in the darkness of her room. This is indeed
wild. But like father, like son.

There's a counterargument: If he was already married,
wouldn't there have been rumors in this town of rumors?
And wouldn't this rumor have reached her by now? But if
she was able to keep her Newar lover secret from the prying

eyes of the world for so long, why would it be inconceivable to think that Tarun has kept a secret mistress or wife somewhere? It could also be that this woman is not originally from here. It could be that she migrated from somewhere else, and there's no one in the city who can identify her. A woman no one knows. A woman who doesn't need anyone else, as she is cared for by a young businessman. She is provided for—food, clothing, jewelry, an occasional trip. A kept wife, or a kept mistress, while Rukma is the official one.

The velocity of this new understanding exhausts her, and she falls asleep.

The sun is streaming brightly through the window when she wakens. She goes down the stairs to discover that Tarun has left for work. Does he stop by his woman's place before he heads to his office, then visit her briefly again in the evening? Or perhaps this morning they are meeting at a temple. He's not religious, but she may be. She could be praying every day that God do something so that she and Tarun may be united fully, as man and wife. But God's intervention is not even necessary. I can make it happen, Rukma thinks, I can play God. I can slip out of the way.

She's going to make is easy for him, for them. Today.

As soon as she has a cup of tea and piece of toast she leaves home, not in her sari but in her pants and shirt. Like the old times. The clothes free her; she hasn't worn them since her marriage was finalized because she thought they wouldn't be appropriate. But who is to stop her now? She's a single woman again. Sanmaya stared at her clothes when she was having breakfast but said nothing.

Rukma is conscious that her fancy pants and tight shirt from her Newar lover days make her look like Sahara, and maybe she is meant to be a Sahara now, unmoored. She will remain single all her life, and she'll try to be happy in her solitude.

She has no idea where she'll look for a room. No longer does she have any romantic notions about living in the city's ancient center with the common folk. But the suburbs don't appeal to her either—she wants to get away now, as far as possible from this house, this type of closed-in, walled house with its rooms of madness and entropy. It certainly didn't help her mother-in-law one bit to be so isolated; she might have been better off wandering the city streets.

She takes a taxi to the Tripureswor area, on an impulse, and she dives into lanes and alleys seeking FOR RENT signs. She finds a few places, and finally one appeals to her. It's a two-room flat at the top of a building. It affords a view of the busy street below, and on the other side there's a school whose yard is filled with screaming, happy children. Nearby is a motorcycle sales and repair shop. She inquires about the rent, then tells the landlady she'll be back in the evening or, at the latest, tomorrow.

Once on the pavement below, she sees him, crossing the street in his suit and tie. He's emerging from a building that has the sign EVEREST FINANCIAL. Her first instinct is to call

out to him, pretend she's a normal wife who has unexpect-
edly, and delightfully, run into her husband. *Fancy meeting
you here!*

Instead, she observes him. In all her meanderings she's
never encountered him like this. He crosses the street, then
opens the door of his car. If he turns his head he'll spot her.
But she knows he won't. And if he does he won't see her
because—and this idea entertains her—she's become face-
less, just another woman standing on the sidewalk. This
idea appeals to her.

She watches Tarun open the door of his car. He tosses
in his briefcase and coat, then loosens his tie and throws it
after them. He is off duty. He doesn't get into the car. He
looks around quickly, then starts up the hill toward Dharahara. She follows.

The crowd thickens near the tower. Now, even if he were
to look back, she'd simply be a face among scores of pedestrians. So strong is her sense of anonymity that when she
looks at her reflection in a storefront window the woman
in pants and shirt who returns her gaze is not someone she
knows. Ahead of her, he passes the tower to his right, and
a short moment later she, too, passes it. He glances at his
watch, and a short moment later she, too, glances at hers.
He stops in front of a tall building, looks to his left and
right, and climbs the stairs at the side of the building.

She waits under the awning of a shop across the street,
watching his white-shirted figure climb the steps leisurely.
It's his second home, after all. His kept wife is waiting for

him upstairs; she may even have cooked something for him. They may be planning an outing tonight.

He's aware of the presence all along, from the moment he throws in his suitcase and his coat and tie into the car in Tripureswor. He doesn't turn to look, but he knows it's there. It follows him as he climbs the hill toward Dharahara. It's not even a real thing—it's just an awareness, literally in the back of his head. This is not the same brooding presence, dark and suffocating, that hovered around him when he followed, incognito, young women around the city—he hasn't followed anyone since he got married. This entity is more awake and intelligent and carries with it a light that's gentle and warm. As he reaches Dharahara, he stifles the urge to look back and see what it is, if the presence is even tangible. But he's afraid that as soon as he swivels his neck, the entity will disappear, and all he'll see is the glum multitude that inhabits the city. He doesn't want to jinx anything, so he keeps his head straight and continues walking. Something is about to happen: he feels it coming. Something is about to break open, and it has to do with the light that's staying close to him, watching, observing. Where was this light thus far in his life? Why let him wander in the torturous landscape of his own mind all these years? He doesn't know the answer.

As he climbs the long staircase to the top, and as he takes out the key, the knowledge dawns on him, gradually: what this force is or, rather, *who* this force is. He doesn't need to look down at the street to confirm: now he's certain who has been following him. His fingers tremble as he inserts the key into the padlock and twists it open. *Don't back out now, don't back out now,* he says to himself. And he has, he recognizes with a painful clarity, no choice but to allow this breakage to happen. He cannot stand in its way.

Below, the corner of Rukma's eyes catches a movement. It's a familiar figure. Didi. Rukma is confused. It's a coincidence: Didi works nearby and is most likely out on an errand that has nothing to do with this building. But this conjecture is quickly abandoned when she sees Didi pause at the bottom of the building to gather her breath, then move toward the stairs.

Do Didi and Tarun meet here, instead of Bangemudha? Is this the house of a relative, perhaps, that Rukma isn't aware of? But something is odd here, something calculated and sinister. It doesn't take her too long to come up with a possibility that jolts her: Didi is in on Tarun's secret. Then in rapid succession, her mind makes leaps. This is also possible: the kept wife or mistress is someone who's been fixed for Tarun by Didi herself, which explains his reverence for Didi and the mild hostility Rukma sensed from Didi toward her. This is also not out of bounds: the mistress is someone from Didi's village, a young woman who came here looking for work and found love. Didi thinks it's not a bad match at all, Tarun and this girl, and she's unhappy that Tarun caved in to Mahesh Uncle to marry someone else.

It makes sense now: Didi didn't attend Tarun's wedding because she doesn't want to recognize Rukma's legitimacy. Tarun's father and Amit and Sumit either don't know about the kept wife, or they're under strict injunctions not to go blabbering. At some point a conclusion could have been reached in that household: let there be an official wife; what difference does it make? Perhaps the stepmother, the fixer of this liaison, has been invited for tea today. The couple upstairs might be eagerly waiting for their favorite mother, their darling.

All these associations and possibilities—all occur in a span of a few seconds, yet they cohere, and they are the only way to make sense of this picture now: Didi climbing up the stairs, only a few minutes after Tarun.

Rukma crosses the street and stands at the bottom of the stairs. In the Japanese garden during their first meeting she'd told Tarun that she wanted to do something that'd shatter the world. Well, this is her opportunity. It'll be quite something to see the shock on their faces. Then she'll bid them goodbye and get out of their way.

On the floor above there's a photocopying shop, then on the next floor another shop or an office. She continues climbing, breathless, until she reaches the top. There's a single room up here from where muted voices are coming. But she's drawn to the wide roof, and the amazing view from here. She can see the white tower of Dharahara up close, even make out the figure of a man at the railing that circles the tower toward the top. Although she can't be sure, it appears the man, his arms on the railing, is also looking down at her. From the rooftop she can see the city spread out before her. Such a ruckus from below rising up to the sky and disappearing. The sky is dark blue, with not even a bird to block the sunrays.

But the voices coming from the room behind her distract her, and she returns to it. There's a small window that hangs low on the side of the room. It's meant to enable a view of the roof, but half of the window is smeared with paint, in a haphazard manner, leaving only a small patch of clear glass. She doesn't know whether the people inside, Didi and Tarun and his kept wife, are aware of her presence on the roof. She doesn't care. The truth will come out, soon enough. She crouches down and listens. She hears a cry, which she takes to be the voice of the kept wife but realizes then that it's the voice of a man, Tarun's, and the cry is of pleasure. Or is it a call for help? She presses her face to the glass.

PART 4

CHAPTER TWENTY-FIVE

SHE HOPES THAT he'll not do anything silly, like jump into the falls. He's gone a bit past the viewing area cordoned off by a railing and is at the farthest edge. He can, if he wants to, plunge into the raging water below.

They've come to this resort town by the lake because she insisted on it. "Come, it'll do us both good," she'd said to him. In the past few days, when on occasion she's been aware of his gaze on her, she's been startled by the depth of shame in his eyes. And at other times he appears resentful. I don't deserve it, she's thought, I should simply leave him, as I was about to in the first place. But when their eyes meet, she smiles, and her smile does something to him: softens him, makes him realize how strong was Didi's grip.

He's beginning to understand the depth of the dark cave in which he's been living.

Didi's whereabouts are unknown. She has simply vanished. She is gone, but her spirit still lingers in Tarun. The Masterji hardly speaks to anyone. Confined to his bed, his attempts at speaking are now limited to his slowly raising his index finger, shaking and trembling, in the air, as though he is driving home a scholarly point. But Rukma infers that the admonishing finger is directed at himself. Rukma doesn't have much respect for him, but when she sees his condition she is overcome with pity. "Baba," she says, smoothing his forehead, and his expression is one of surprise, a man who doesn't understand why he's receiving any affection. He doesn't mention Didi, but a couple of times he has whispered a name that sounds like Apsara. Rukma goes to Bangemudha every few days to spend time with this family, which now consists of the Masterji and Sumit, who still smiles, but when he's caught unawares, there's some sadness in his eyes. This house needs a woman's presence in order to heal, she's been thinking lately, and although she hopes her visits help, she is also considering finding a suitable wife for Sumit. She doesn't want the boy's happiness to turn into loneliness so early in his life. Sumit is a devoted son, cooks for, feeds, and helps bathe his father, then goes to work. He teaches at a nearby school and is a popular teacher. But life is becoming hard for him, and Rukma believes that a female companion will ameliorate some of his difficulties. He blushes and says, "No, *bhauju*, no," when Rukma raises the topic.

Amit is now a full-fledged drug addict. He came to Lazimpat one day. Gaunt, barely able to hold himself up, he argued with the guard who took him to be a man of the streets. Amit kept telling the guard he was Tarun's brother, so Rukma guessed who he was and asked the guard to let him in. She took Amit to the dining room table. Sanmaya was not pleased, even after she was told who Amit was. When Rukma asked her to bring tea, she went to the kitchen reluctantly, mumbling.

Amit asked Rukma to come closer, making her blanch at his foul breath. "I've known there was something all along," he says. His mustache was already gray, even though he was just a year or two older than Tarun. His eyes were the color of drain water, and his clothes hung loosely on his body. He gave the impression that at any moment he could fold onto himself, like a cardboard façade. A thin strip of saliva ran from a corner of his mouth. "She looked at him wrongly when we first came to the city. I used to bully him, but I was only a child. Her anger was . . ." He struggled with the words.

"If you suspected it, why did you keep quiet?"

"Well, didn't he want some of it?" He shook his head and gave a soft, deprecatory laugh. "He was so precious he didn't know what he was getting into."

Sanmaya thinks Didi will return. "A woman like that," she says, "will never be satisfied with the damage she's done.

She'll come back for more." She hasn't been given all the details, but she's heard whispers between Mahesh Uncle and Rukma and seen Tarun's forlorn look. Sanmaya has become even older; she stoops more, and her movements around the house have slowed. She wheezes when she has to go up and down the stairs. Yet her eyes are as alert as ever, and, to Rukma's surprise, she's remained cheerful as the days have passed.

It is Mahesh Uncle who seems to have been hit the hardest. After Rukma told him what she had seen, he became galvanized. He had been lying in bed when she entered his room and informed him. He hastily sat up and began asking her questions, some of which she could answer and some she couldn't. How long had this been going on? She didn't know. Where was this place? Near Dharahara. Was she sure it was Didi? Yes. Was she sure she saw what she did? Yes.

"I'll take care of it," he said, and she left his room so he could change.

From what she could gather—Mahesh Uncle was somewhat secretive—he went straight to Bangemudha and confronted Didi. The Masterji was home; Sumit was not. Mahesh Uncle challenged Didi in the kitchen, within the Masterji's earshot. Mahesh Uncle didn't reveal to Rukma what he told Didi, but Rukma imagined threats of the police and jail, of out-and-out exposure, and perhaps there was also a bribe—there was an envelope filled with money when Mahesh Uncle left. What was Didi's price for going away, for vanishing from the lives of those she'd ruined?

But Rukma isn't convinced that money was a major impetus for Didi to leave. If she were after money, she'd have milked Tarun dry by now; she'd not have been satisfied with the small amounts he'd given her. And Rukma also has a tough time believing that Didi had been intimidated by Mahesh Uncle. So what was it? Was it a realization, a dim awareness, perhaps, of the harm she had done? Was it also a recognition that her time was up with Tarun? Was it the force of Mahesh Uncle's goodness—the same goodness that had taken a near-suicidal mother and a bewildered child into his home—that finally had shifted something in Didi, weakened that part of her that had made her do what she did with Tarun? Rukma's thoughts become tied up in intricate knots as she finds herself dwelling on Didi, her history, and her motives. Now when Rukma recalls the scene she witnessed in that tower-top room, she sees herself as higher up than she actually had been, so high that the room floats in the clouds, with people crawling like ants down on the streets.

Soon after Didi's departure, Mahesh Uncle became bedridden with strong bouts of fever, draining much of his energy. He blamed himself, Rukma knew, for the grave injustice that had been occurring, as he put it, under his own nose. Mahesh Uncle mumbled something about "only a boy," and the regret in his voice deepened. He was the one who'd suggested that the two of them go to Pokhara for vacation, "do what needs to be done." To Rukma he seemed to be saying: *You are free to leave him, leave me, leave this family whenever you wish. After all this, no one in their right mind can expect you to stay.*

Rukma has seriously considered leaving. Even when she's in the midst of trying to make things work, when she's putting some effort into consoling, rectifying, into healing broken spirits, the urge has been strong in her, to simply get up and walk away, just as she used to feel when working at Swarga. But this desire to abandon is more expansive. It's to "walk away from it all," a phrase that has been running through her mind like a private chant: her husband, this family, the other family, her parents, this city, this country.

She can abandon him right now as he's staring into the frothing, gushing water below. She can go out to the street, take a taxi to the bus stand, and hop on a bus for the border, a distance of only a few hours. She can stay in a hotel across the border in India, then tomorrow ride on a train to a bigger city. She can look for a job and live a life of secrecy, not revealing who she is to anyone. Incognito. She can remain elusive and unknown.

But she has already woven a pattern here, among these people, and if she leaves, this pattern will come undone and fall apart. Mahesh Uncle—he gets sustenance from her presence, from the simple fact that, despite everything, she is still around. There's also the Masterji. A faint disgust rises up in her when she visits Bangemudha, but she also can't help thinking that the man has suffered enough. What greater punishment than to live with the knowledge of his cowardice in the face of what Didi was doing to his own son? His mind will not stop tormenting him—the very mind that brought him fame at one point—and he will not stop raising his finger at himself. Then there is Sumit, who has begun to look up to her, his face brightening every time she visits, his eyes soft and moist when they land upon her. She already feels a sisterly affection for him, and wouldn't he be filled with disappointment if she left?

Finally, what about this man, Tarun, standing a few feet away from her? After Rukma's discovery, after he was "caught red-handed"—Rukma's words when she's angry, feels trapped—his turbulent emotions surfaced. At night he thrashes in bed, like a body in the throes of exorcism. Twice he's wept in her arms.

What about all these people? By going away she'll be announcing that they don't matter. But she wants to believe that they do. That at some level all the small moments with Mahesh Uncle, with Sanmaya, Sumit, the Masterji, with Tarun, they amount to something. That they accrue.

For now, she has only this instant to take care of, so she goes and stands next to him. It's not very deep below, but the water swirls about at a speed that's dizzying. He's not looking at the water; his eyes are fixed on the horizon. When did it start? She's wondered about this many, many times. What was the first instance like, when Didi touched him with improper desire? Tears have come to her eyes when she's pictured it. Oh, he was only a child, only a child!

"What are you thinking?" she asks him.

"My mother," he says. "She was such a weak woman." It's said without any rancor or disappointment. There's even a hint of compassion in his voice.

She searches for something to say. "Come," she says at last, "let's return to the hotel."

In the taxi she clasps his hand. He looks at her, shyly, as if he is just beginning to get to know her. "I'm glad we came to Pokhara," he says. "It was good to get away from all that noise, that confusion." He squeezes her hand. "Get away with you."

That evening—their last night in Pokhara—they watch a dinner dance show on the lawn of the hotel. The final performance is of a masked dancer, who startles the guests by running toward them from the kitchen area rather than appearing on the stage. The dancer's movements are robust, even aggressive. He is accompanied by the beats of drums and cymbals coming from the shadows. He prances from table to table, especially targeting children. There are gasps, laughter, even whimpers of complaints at this invasion. But mostly the guests are awed by the electric charge he's brought to the evening, to what had otherwise been a string of lackluster ethnic dances. "Lakhey! Lakhey!" someone shouts.

The lakhey stops at Tarun and Rukma's table. His engorged eyes are focused on Tarun. "The lakhey is going to eat him," a voice says loudly, with relish, then the air becomes silent. The lakhey leans over and inches his face closer to Tarun's until their noses are nearly touching. All color has drained from Tarun's face. Alarmed, Rukma is about to rebuke him, ask him to move on, when he takes Tarun's hands and, with gentle nods of his head, urges Tarun to stand. Tarun appears paralyzed. Sweat dots his forehead. Then, his frightened eyes affixed to the lakhey's face, he slowly gets up from his chair.

The lakhey leads Tarun to the open area in the center of the lawn, where he begins to dance with him. Tarun is hesitant at first. He looks ready to bolt. Then his shoulders loosen, and he distrustfully shakes his body. Soon, his movements become more vigorous.

The crowd is whooping and clapping and hollering. At one point he turns toward Rukma, and under the lawn's reddish lamp, he looks fierce. He pivots toward the lakhey.

ACKNOWLEDGMENTS

I am deeply grateful to my parents for sending me off to America and giving me the freedom to pursue my art.

My teachers in Hawaii, in particular Robbie Shapard and the late Ian MacMillan, and the brilliant folks at the journal *Manoa,* were instrumental in my development as a writer.

Many thanks to my friends and students at Indiana University for their support.

Eric Simonoff and Claudia Ballard at WME believed in this book right from the beginning. I could not have found better agents.

I am thrilled to have discovered the wonderful Soho Press, and a smart and caring editor in Mark Doten. Thanks also to Rupa Publication for making this book available in South Asia.

None of this would be possible without my wife Babita, whose generosity over the years has made all of my books real.

Made in the USA
Coppell, TX
10 June 2021